Is It Just Me?

And other stories from my unbelievable, hilarious, ridiculous life.

HELEN ROW TOEWS

VOLUME ONE

Copyright © 2019 by Helen Row Toews

All rights reserved.
This book or any portion thereof may not be reproduced or used in any manner whatsoever without the expressed written permission of the publisher except for the use of brief quotation in a book review.

Printed in North America
First Edition, Volume One, 2020

Prairie Wool Books
Is It Just Me?
Volume One

Cover design by Todd Toews

myprairiewool.com

This book is dedicated to my wonderful children:
Chris, Rebecca, Justin and Aliyah.
You will always be the best part of my life.

ACKNOWLEDGMENTS

I would like to thank a few people without whom this book would not be possible.

First of all my husband Tom for his love and understanding as he puts up with my long hours at the computer.

My dear family and friends for their belief in me and unflagging support along the way. You know who you are.

My stepson Todd Toews for his artistic expertise in creating the cover and helping me in many other ways too numerous to mention. These books could not have been done without you.

Melanie Toews, my step-daughter-in-law for all of her support and kindness.

Mike D'Amour, for starting me down this path and advising along the way.

And Dad, who has been my strength and inspiration without end.

Love you Dad.

TABLE OF CONTENTS

Constant Need of Improvement	1
Looking For Love?	4
Out of the Mouths of Babes	7
Cattlemen!	10
Is It Just Me?	13
Me and the Lizard	17
Is There a Seamstress In the House?	21
Kids Do the Darndest Things	25
Rise and Shine!	28
Manure Capers	31
Who Says Cows are Dull?	35
Enough With the Cats Already!	38
Fire Hazards	42
Let Them Eat Cake	45
Mouse Tales	49
Stuck On the Prairies	52
Shut Up and Do It!	56
Wild Encounters?	60
An Apple A Day	64
Dear Abby (Helen)	68
Lessons Learned	71
Never Enough Time	74
A Sporting Event	78
Absolutely Shocking	81
Age Is Only A Number	84
Beach Bums	87
Appearance vs. Reality	90

Hair Dos (and Don'ts)	93
I Go Out Walkin' After Midnight	96
Rednecks	100
Signs of the Times	103
The Gift of Family	106
Teenagers!	110
You're Only as Old as You Feel	113
Welcome Back	117
Tammy?	120
Nuggets Of Gold	123
You Are Entering the Hunt Zone	127
Women Drivers	131
Second-hand Style	135
Halloween Hullabaloo	138
Where's My Cane?	141
Talkin' Trash	144
A True Cowboy	147
Sing Me Back Home	150
Ignorance Is Bliss	153
Is There A Problem?	156
Those Who Live In Glass Houses	159
A Series Of Unpleasant Events	162
Tell Me A Story	166
Keeping It Real	169
Lost and Found	172
Filling the Cookie Jar	175
Trouble for Santa	178

Constant Need of Improvement

Whenever January looms on our horizon, we look ahead with hope for a bright New Year and enjoy full expectation of good things to come.

This in spite of that annoying question ringing in our ears: "Have you made any New Year's resolutions?"

Roughly 45 per cent of people do, of one sort or another, but only about eight per cent are successful in achieving their goals.

I'm not sure how these statistics are determined, but it sounds about right. Many plans are for self-improvement, most notably weight reduction and fitness. According to the proprietors of gymnasiums and diet centers, we are in constant need of improvement, but apparently it's never more urgent than during the winter months.

This irritating query into our resolve, coupled with television ads mercilessly attacking our slovenly ways, makes a person feel we had better do something about it— and quick.

Let's take a moment to consider the finer points of such campaigns for our betterment.

I suppose this time of year is synonymous with over-indulgence and sloth. Advertisers know full well we've taken an extra slab of pie or pounded back enough cheesecake to tip a boat. They count on our guilt over past gluttony, and our naive faith in their promise of quick and effortless weight loss.

They're good at it too! In January I received a letter from a weight-loss company that addressed me with easy familiarity and expressed sincere regret over my unfortunate weight gain and unsightly muffin-top. It pointed out that friends have noticed my lack of confidence in social situations and mentioned how apparent it was to them my old sparkle was gone due to this excess poundage. Thankfully, the company kindly extended its hand of friendship, assuring me those days would be long gone once enrollment took effect and I received my first shipment of "fat burning" pills.

My question is: How did they know? Are there spies in our midst? Was I secretly filmed hefting an extra-large salted caramel latte to my lips as I rolled out the drive-thru?

Moreover, how can we chocoholics be expected to make responsible choices when so many goodies are promoted during the holidays?

Last year, minding my own business, I strolled through a department store on my way to peruse its selection of reduced price mittens. (It made sense at the time, don't give me any trouble.)

Unexpectedly, a sonorous loudspeaker announcement

cut into my thoughts.

"All holiday chocolates, nuts and candy have been reduced to 70 per cent off!"

Sigh. Two factors come into play here: one is my well-established affection for chocolate and nuts, and the second is my love of a bargain. Some may use the word "cheap" as a descriptor, but I prefer to think of myself as thrifty.

My daughter often caustically remarks we'd own nothing if it didn't first have either a red tag or a yellow label, but she's young and foolish so we can disregard her bitter lament. Nonetheless, it was poor judgment indeed that caused me to scurry toward the promised spoils.

Telling myself I was purchasing these items to share with deserving loved ones at home; I stuffed my basket and proudly lugged them into the house later that day.

I gained ten pounds before the month was out.

Based on this revealing information, I am hardly one to offer advice concerning New Year's resolutions aimed at getting in shape. Perhaps it's best to simply wish your health and happiness in the coming year and end on the insightful words of Mark Twain:

"Now is the accepted time to make your regular annual good resolutions. Next week you can begin paving hell with them as usual."

Looking for Love?

"Find love this Valentine's Day", television ads exhort.

Apparently you have only yourself to blame if you're alone these days. There appears to be an Internet dating site for everyone. It's become a whole new world out there with the advent of technology. For better or worse Internet dating has become a part of life as we know it. So, with this quest in mind, I've decided to tap out a few pointers for any gentleman interested in attracting a lovely lady.

When a close friend of mine was young, her father was a strong, stoic farmer who, as a rule, didn't have much to say about her admirers. Nonetheless, I remember him breaking his self-imposed silence concerning one fellow she dated for a while: a pale, fresh-faced youth with a slender sort of build.

Early one evening, after a light rain, his vehicle spun out in a rather slick area of their driveway. His feeble attempts to extricate this car from the mud left her father pulling on his jacket at the door to go help, shaking his head and muttering, "That boy couldn't carry a pail of water across the yard."

#1 Be able to negotiate the expanse of a backyard whilst toting a reasonably sized container of liquid.

I was set up on a blind date in the late 90s with a pleasant fellow who unfortunately stepped out of his car wearing a pale blue leisure suit made entirely of Fortrel. What is Fortrel you may ask? Nay, what is a pale blue leisure suit? These words should never grace the same sentence, let alone the same man. It was an unholy union in the 70s and should never have made it to the 90s.

#2 Dress styles popular two or more decades ago are NOT encouraged. And for gosh sake let the Fortrels live in peace!

In 2004, a friend agreed to a blind date with what proved to be a really lovely person. However, she almost canceled after chatting on the phone and learning several unfortunate facts. First advising her he would be able to arrive in a timely fashion at the cafe since his parents (with whom he lived) recently bought new tires for his '73 Datsun, he then happily divulged how people always thought he and his father were brothers. He was 35—the father was 72.

#3 Never give away too much information up front. Particularly if it concerns impoverished living arrangements or premature aging.

Another acquaintance of mine once asked a colleague to attend a dance with him and his wife and me. It was a thinly veiled attempt at matchmaking.

At the appointed time, the potential suitor strode to the door, hastily raking fingers through his hair in an attempt to smooth out a heavily oiled coiffure. Nevertheless, it wasn't his hair, laced with pomade, my startled eyes were drawn to. It was the many tiny tufts of blood-dotted toilet paper stuck to his face from which I was unable to peel my gaze.

"Oh," he said with a sheepish grin, rubbing the dried blood and paper briskly from his cheeks. "I stuck those there after I shaved off my warts. Guess I forgot them."

#4 Any and all discussion of warts or the removal thereof is strictly prohibited! Trust me on this people...no one needs or wants to hear about it.

Wherever you live or whatever background you come from, a desire to find true love and form a lasting relationship with that special someone is something we all share. And, despite poking a little fun at it all, I firmly believe in the old adage that states: "It's what's inside the person that counts."

Good luck!

Out of the Mouths of Babes

As the bus rumbled down the road last week—it was Valentine's Day—I overheard an exchange between two of the students seated behind me.

I drive a school bus and often catch enlightening snippets of conversation from my vantage point behind the wheel. This one brought a laugh to my lips at the time, but afterward I got thinking how truly wise these words were.

I believe the conversation might be amusing for us all to hear, but encouraging too. Sometimes little children really can lead the way.

It was an exciting day for the young ones, and spirits were high. A number of them had clambered eagerly on board, then paused to thrust out slightly crumpled Valentine cards for me as well.

I even received a heart- shaped Jell-O jiggler—eat your hearts out people!

Gleaming eyes eagerly awaited my response, and I was careful not to let them down. Tiny faces beamed with pleasure as they took their seats and we roared off.

Quite a few youngsters, aged five to six, ride with me each day. They sit in the front seats where pint-size winter boots swish back and forth rapidly as the children weigh in on a variety of, sometimes bizarre, subjects.

At one of my stops a family of three race one another to the wide, swinging door and pile up the steps.

The eldest of them is a boy named Carson Irwin, who always seats himself among these young children in order to chat with me.

This never fails to create a hum of excitement. Although he likely wouldn't appreciate this descriptor, Carson is a sweetheart. He has a kind and loving heart; always inquiring into the health and happiness of these small ones.

He asks pertinent questions with the utmost seriousness, then patiently listens to the youngsters' garbled answers, nodding his head in understanding, or voicing appropriate shock and alarm over their wild stories.

He also loves a good laugh. Carson and I often share a giggle over some funny situation or other.

On this particular day, the little girls were all a-flutter as they clutched their Valentines and chattered busily of the upcoming festivities at school.

"Do you have all your Valentine's ready to give away Carston?" a bright, squeaky voice asked from behind him, mispronouncing his name. She peeked around the seat to deliver this very important question and smiled engagingly, despite the lack of several front teeth.

He turned towards the upturned faces, all anxiously waiting for his reply and answered gravely, "No, I don't have

Valentines for anyone." The eyes around him slowly grew big as saucers with disbelief as he continued, "I'm 12 now. Don't ya think I'm a bit old for that?"

The resulting silence was palpable. They sat, rigid in their seats, aghast at this dreadful revelation.

Suddenly, the same tiny girl leapt to her feet, indignation bringing a rosy flush to her cheeks. Chestnut curls bounced, eyes flashed as she shot back, "YOU'RE NEVER TOO OLD TO LOVE PEOPLE!"

Chuckling, I put the bus in gear and pulled out the driveway, mulling over her words.

How true this simple phrase was, and is.

Transpose the word *old* for a multitude of others and it works just as well.

We should never be too rich or poor, too tired, busy or distracted to love people. Showing love for family, friends or our fellow man can be expressed in many ways besides sentimental cards, and should never be limited to one day a year—or to the young.

What stronger force exists in this world? What one is more essential to our very survival?

Troubled times of every sort have been with us since the beginning of this old world, but love never fails.

Out of the mouths of babes.

Cattlemen!

Having a father who's a cattleman has often created humorous situations.

When I was heavily pregnant with my first child, Dad and my brother Bill were in the thick of calving, and Dad was pretty preoccupied with the welfare of the animals.

However, he caught my eye one morning as I lumbered through the kitchen after a visit.

"I want to tell you something important," he declared, motioning me closer.

He glanced furtively from side to side, rubbed his grizzled jaw in some agitation, and then stated clearly and distinctly, "Calves don't do well on milk replacement." With this cryptic remark he nodded his head sagely. Clearly his job was done.

"Glad we had this little talk Helen," he said, clapping me heartily on the back. *What little talk*, I asked myself as he briskly stepped away.

Men of my father's generation were not known to speak at length on feminine subjects. This was his way of telling me I should be nursing my baby. If it's good for the cow, by golly it's good for the girl!

I unfortunately developed mastitis after the birth of my son. It was a nasty, painful business and required an immediate trip to my doctor. Sadly, my husband had our only vehicle at work so I called Dad.

Sure I'll take you," he said, "but it'll have to be in the grain truck. I'm haulin' a load into town after lunch." Peachy. Only I'd be driven to seek therapeutic treatment in a loaded utility vehicle.

Anyway, Mom looked after the baby and I dragged my aching, miserable carcass up the steps of the massive vehicle and sprawled across the vinyl bench seat. Sweat rolled from my brow with the effort of these small movements; I had a temperature of 103 and felt like I'd been hit by a train.

Too weak to complain, I moaned pitifully from my prone position across the cold, hard seat. A pile of old tractor rags, saturated with the scent of diesel and grease, lay beneath my head. A hammer and a can of staples rattled on the floor beneath my feet, along with a bit of barbed wire that angrily jabbed at my ankles, but I was past caring.

Dad whistled a happy tune as we rumbled into town, hitting each and every pothole the road had to offer.

Several surprised faces appeared at the window of the medical facility as we pulled up with a squeal of brakes and a light showering of oats.

I pushed myself upright, with difficulty, and brushed a few grains of petrified wheat from my cheek where they'd become embedded en route.

With glazed eyes I reached for the door as Dad leaned toward me and kindly patted my hand.

He grinned cheerfully into my flushed face.

"Don't worry honey. You'll be fine," he said.

"I haven't lost a cow yet."

Is It Just Me?

Is it just me, or do you find teenagers these days often have a better vehicle than the one you drive?

I mean, great if their parents can afford one, but there's just some element of it all that irks me.

When a young man, barely able to see over the steering wheel, sweeps past me in an enormous new truck on his way to school, I'm vaguely irritated, and find myself thinking back to a time when I was in my teens.

There was no shiny new vehicle for me parked in the driveway. My parents did what they could, and I appreciate their sacrifices more and more as I get older, but I wasn't handed a new car—neither was my brother Bill.

Of course, all young people don't have new vehicles.

Take my son, Justin, for instance. Although not a teen any longer, he's a fine example of starting out with very little, and building up from there.

He motors about the countryside in a car, which qualifies for antique status; a 1982 Firebird. I asked him to take my vehicle into town for some repairs a few weeks back, which left me to drive his.

Holy doodlecakes!

Some months ago, with an eye towards restoration, he completely gutted it, but sadly funds ran low, leaving much of the dash, the console and the backseat, in his trunk. To say the interior is grim and austere is understating things by quite a bit.

As we walked towards the 'Bird, Justin dropped the keys into my outstretched palm, mentioning casually, "You might wanna bundle up. There's no heat."

He left, hands shoved in his pockets, whistling a cheerful tune, as his aged mother prepared to clamber behind the wheel.

Hunkering low to the ground, I shuffled my feet out well past any reasonable center of gravity, sidled up to the open door, and flung myself within.

You've heard people say their vehicle sits low to the ground? They have no flippin' idea.

The clearance under this monster from Detroit was approximately two centimeters. (I swear I felt gravel crunching directly beneath my posterior as I later rolled down the road).

Swinging the door shut, I briefly glanced at the dog that stood outside absentmindedly licking the glass. She looked down at me questioningly before I leaned back and passed from view, backward onto the suddenly flattened seat.

Where were the controls to move the blasted thing forward and upright? Great, there weren't any.

I lay recumbent, staring at the bare, metal roof.

Good. Bloody. Grief!

I texted my son, holding the phone over my face while I typed these words of incredulity. Stretching out a hesitant toe I could just reach the pedals, and if I gripped the steering wheel hard whilst leveraging myself upright, it was almost possible to make out the dim outline of a road through the frosty window.

Mercifully, I only had to get to our nearest town.

Apparently there was a way to raise the seat, but I couldn't find it. If I'd simply flattened myself prostrate into the snow outside the door and scrabbled around under the bucket seat in the nameless bits of rubbish lurking there in the dark, I was assured it would have been found. (I feel so darn dumb).

Nonetheless, the trip was made safely, as I'm sure you've surmised.

It was an interesting journey, as I can't say I ever operated a motor vehicle lying down before. My passage through town was uneventful too, although a few interested bystanders did pause to stare, as a seemingly driver-less car rumbled past.

They might also have wondered why it constantly signaled a left turn. I wasn't aware, but once on, the light failed to cancel; soundlessly indicating my intention to exit the road for a mile-and-a-half.

In hindsight, this may not have been the right incident to cite in order to prove my case.

However, I still maintain kids these days have nicer cars than me.

Justin's was an exception.

Me and the Lizard

The shed was full. Happy cows lay deep in oat straw chewing their cuds as brother Bill quietly moved among them, checking for signs of calving.

It was a placid scene of contentment after the evening chores, and as I stood there watching all the mouths moving steadily, a memory floated back of other munching mouths.

It was of a wedding that took place in Edmonton, Alberta quite a few years ago.

I didn't know the bride all that well, but she asked me to attend, and sing a special song after the ceremony.

She greeted me from her dining table with an anxious look and a distracted wave as I entered her home that morning. A stylist bent over the bride's platinum hair; teasing it into a frothy halo which framed her darkly tanned features.

Five separate headdresses were then fixed into the resulting fluff. A diamond tiara, rhinestone headband, two strands of pearls, three pink flowers, and a sequin encrusted comb were all artfully arranged with the aid of enough hairspray to smother a horse.

The bride-to-be turned to admire the effect in a mirror

the stylist held out. This woman lived a life of excess. Let's call her Mazy.

Brushing past her fiancée's three foot salamander—sorry, I've been corrected on that, it was an iguana—who lay across the back of a sofa, Mazy swept from the room to begin careful application of cosmetics in her boudoir. (Not everyone has a boudoir—she did).

The stylist exited the premises with a sigh, and I was left with the reptile—great!

I perched on the edge of the couch and we contemplated one another quietly for a time, each lost in thought. I wondered why the heck I'd been told to arrive early only to spend quality time with an enormous green lizard, and he wondered if he could snare the lazy fly that circled over my head.

I quickly moved away.

Unbeknownst to me, this is where the trouble started. Mazy had been suffering with nerves, and during her time alone in the boudoir, had resorted to self-medicating with Valium, which is never a good thing.

A limo majestically rolled in two hours later, and Mazy's teenage daughter sprinted up the sidewalk.

"Where's Mom?" she called brightly, "It's time to leave." The lizard and I were blandly watching old Gilligan's Island reruns and I glanced up with a shrug.

The teen rushed to her mother's bedroom door and rapped vigorously.

"Mom!" No answer. More knocking ensued and then a frantic rattling of the knob—now even the lizard was concerned. The girl ran to the kitchen, snatched up a butter knife and deftly picked the lock, but something still prevented her entry.

BONK! BONK! BONK! She banged the door repeatedly into some strange obstruction on the other side, as she continued to call her tardy parent.

Abruptly, the portal was flung wide to reveal her mother slumped beside it on the floor where she had expired—before the repeated pounding on her forehead woke her.

The rhinestone headband hung crazily over one eye and several dark marks were materializing on her brow. Somehow, we got her into the limo and off to the church.

It was some nut in the foyer who really clinched the day by offering the entire wedding party a stick of Wrigley's gum.

Taking my place on the platform, I watched in horror as each smartly dressed attendant, chewing loudly, marched down the aisle.

Finally, Mazy unsteadily entered the sanctuary.

She stared disinterestedly through glazed, heavy lidded eyes at her waiting groom.

Finally, after a certain amount of urging from concerned bystanders, she launched off toward him.

Her hair was matted, flat on one side from her time spent prostrate on the carpet, mascara stained her cheeks and the headband still hung low over one eye, but she chawed purposefully on her gum as she swayed slowly down the aisle.

The betrothed said their vows between chews, and successfully tied the knot.

Suddenly, it was my big moment. The group turned toward me, each mouth chomping expectantly as I stepped to the podium, cleared my throat, looked out upon the dazed assembly and sang, "This is the Day the Lord Hath Made".

What a memory.

Is There a Seamstress in the House?

I'd have made a crummy pioneer woman.

Oh, I could've cooked and cleaned alright, and milking cows and caring for livestock wouldn't have been a problem. Gardening and putting up preserves are chores I enjoy—I didn't say I was good at them.

I'm actually quite fond of wood stoves, and washing clothes by hand would have been hard work but doable, if I had enough time.

Nope, it's sewing and mending clothes for the family I would've failed miserably at. (Also, the slaughter of fluffy barnyard creatures and their later disembowelment—but that's another story.)

In point of fact, my lack of ability in this womanly art of sewing was illustrated quite recently. One morning last week I crawled from my bed, squinted blearily at the luminous numbers on the bedside clock and groaned.

I felt blah. When this happens I always find myself anxiously scanning the closet for a familiar purple dress. Actually, calling it a dress might be a bit grand. It's more of an attractive sack; a vast swath of material which clings to my shoulders and falls in heavy, unflattering folds to my knees. Haute couture it's not, but it's my friend.

Dragging the outfit over my head, I surveyed the results

in a full length mirror. As mentioned, it hung shapelessly, much like the barrel on straps you might see sported by rodeo clowns as they flounce about in front of a bull.

Yes! This was the look I was going for. Sadly, on closer inspection, I noticed a previous tear across the chest had gotten worse, making it impossible to wear again.

"Crud," I said aloud, turning to scrabble through a nearby drawer.

Unfortunately, this favored garment had seen a lot of use and was literally coming apart at the seams.

A woman handy with needle and thread might have repaired these small flaws. A woman who slogged through three years of high school sewing class could probably have fixed it in a jiffy. A woman whose father gifted her one Christmas with a sewing machine—OK, you get the picture.

So did I?

Heck no! Triumphantly I drew a scarf from the bureau and arranged it strategically across the bodice.

Sewing is for chumps. I smiled, then rushed to grab my coat.

In a related development later that morning at work, I distractedly smoothed my hands over the beloved sack while straightening up from a desk.

To my horror the entire bottom section of the garment

soundlessly parted company from the top and floated gracefully toward the floor.

My shins were now festooned in a garland of tatty purple cloth. Snatching the frayed material up, threads fluttering, I scooted hurriedly down the corridor for my stash of safety pins before anyone could witness my disarray. I roughly tacked it together, but as I reached to put away the pins an ominous rending sound was heard.

Further tears had appeared across the front and I spent the remainder of my day dressed in little more than shreds.

The purple sack has given up the ghost and shall be seen no more. Sigh.

Mrs. Brown could've told you this would happen.

She was my Home Ec. teacher in high school.

After the aforementioned three years of sewing classes, two wrap skirts and a pillowcase later, I remained utterly useless.

She did her best to drum it into me, but it was hopeless.

I met her some 20 years later in the local mall, where, unbelievably, she addressed me by name.

I was gobsmacked! She must have taught 15 or 20 years before me, and afterwards probably 10 more. How many students had passed through her door? How could she possibly remember my name?

"Oh that's easy," she laughed.

Her honest brown eyes crinkled as a grin lit up her face: "You were the worst student I've ever had."

So there you have it; proof positive that if I'd been a pioneer, my family would have been forced to skulk throughout the countryside wearing nothing but sackcloth and ashes.

Bring on the 21st century!

Kids Do the Darndest Things

Who out there remembers a program, on both TV and radio, called "Kids Say the Darndest Things!" hosted by Art Linkletter?

He put regular people (especially kids) at ease in front of a microphone, asked them simple questions, and received hilarious answers.

I often think of that program during the course of my workday as bus driver and education assistant. However, I could add to the original title because kids also *do* the darndest things.

One afternoon I strode around a corner near the gymnasium at our local school.

It had been a busy morning and my thoughts were preoccupied with the task ahead as I hurried toward a classroom.

So preoccupied that I almost fell over a young lad who hunkered outside the boy's bathroom, howling in misery. Lurching to a halt, I knelt down to inquire what terrible calamity had befallen him.

He turned brimming blue eyes up to mine, drew a long, ragged breath, and wordlessly extended a tiny fist.

Now, if a person were able to stop time at moments such as these, and step back for one considering instant, a person might not react so rashly as to accept this unknown object of grief that was offered under duress.

A person, able to keep a cool, rational head about them, might not live to regret such impulsive acts of blind trust, especially when it comes to small, weeping, six year old boys.

Naturally, this wise person I speak of was not me.

The little fellow released the item into my outstretched hand and between sobs, began to explain the whole miserable business. "Mrs. Toews … my flashlight … broke and will never … work again."

Sharing the sad reality brought forth a fresh volley of crying and his shoulders shuddered convulsively as he strove to control his emotion. Streams of tears ran unchecked down glistening cheeks and he brushed them away with a sleeve. "Maybe you … could fix it?" he said, eyes pleading.

"Maybe so," I smiled, turning my attention to the problematic thing I clasped. Uncurling my fingers I beheld a tiny metal flashlight attached to a short, silver key chain. But wait, something was odd with this scenario.

"Mathew, why is it so wet?"

I feigned nonchalance, but suddenly felt a wave of impending doom clutch my heart. He paused and his mop of golden curls bent close as he prodded the trinket now lying in a pool of water on my palm.

"Well, that's why it's not working," he wailed in an aggrieved tone, clearly annoyed with my dull witted lack of understanding. "It fell in the toilet when I was going poop and it's broken forever!"

I can tell you in all honestly, as I gazed at my dripping hand, I could easily have shed a tear myself at that point. It's certainly true; you never know what may happen next when you work with children each day.

They say, and do, the darndest things.

Rise and Shine

Ever had one of those mornings when you know you should have just lurked in bed? I experienced one recently and have decided to take you along for the whole miserable re-enactment.

Lucky you.

The morning started off fairly well. Oh sure, there's always the anxiety associated with packing lunches for work and school, gobbling breakfast, and then trying to whip myself into some sort of presentable shape for work (not an easy task I can assure you).

No, the trouble began when I slid my feet into my husband's steel-toed work boots and clumped out the door in bathrobe and curlers to start the bus.

Driving a school bus is my occupation and, like the U.S. mail: "Neither snow, nor rain, nor heat, nor gloom of night stays these couriers from the swift completion of their appointed rounds".

A bit dramatic, but you get the picture.

It had been warm the previous afternoon; the snow had melted, then frozen into a sheet of ice. During the night a westerly wind picked up and polished the land with sifting snow until it gleamed.

Sadly, I hadn't noticed, or things might have ended quite differently. Instead, I jogged heavily down the incline, gathering momentum with every step until suddenly I couldn't stop, my feet flew up to meet me, and I measured my length across the frozen wasteland with a resounding WHUMP.

Thanks to Newton's laws of physics—dealing with acceleration and force, not to mention a slippery slope—I skimmed along for quite some time before grinding slowly to a halt. A protracted interval then ensued, marked only by the groans of a middle-aged woman struggling to breathe.

However, as the first cold rays of dawn illuminated me, spread-eagle-on-the-driveway-beside-our-busy-thoroughfare, I gathered the presence of mind to wonder what might occur if I was spotted from the road, and someone drove in to see if I were dead.

If they did, it wouldn't play out the way these things do in movies. It never does for me. On the silver screen a handsome, brawny man would leap from his expensive automobile and rush to my aid. With a dazzling, but sympathetic smile, he'd bend anxiously over my perfectly made-up features and artfully arranged hair, gather up my slight, almost waif-like body, and lift me effortlessly into his masterful arms.

Naturally, I'd be wearing fluffy, high-heeled slippers and a pink, diaphanous peignoir set which would flutter attractively in the breeze, as he'd purposefully march to the sanctuary of my door. Once there, he'd take his leave only after assuring himself I was sufficiently recovered to carry on alone. Doubtless, he'd then bow low, kissing my lily-white hand before motoring away with a caring gesture of farewell.

My reality, however, would likely involve a 90-pound weakling (as featured in old Charles Atlas ads) clambering unhurriedly from some rattletrap vehicle, to prod my lifeless bulk with the toe of his boot. He'd bend to peer into my puffy, gasping face, scrubbed clean of all artifice apart from the unpleasant remnants of yesterday's mascara, and would visibly recoil. Curlers would be strewn about me in the snow like tiny fragments of flotsam after a damaged freighter disappears beneath the waves.

My fuzzy purple housecoat, warmed by body heat, would have become one with the ice beneath it, and I imagined my savior chipping it free with an old shovel I keep nearby to dispose of dog crap.

Finally, amid much awkward scrabbling and heated exchange, he'd drag me upright by the scruff of the neck before exiting the yard without so much as a backward glance.

Alone, I'd skitter to the bus, feeling like a bloody fool. How nice. But, enough foolish visions.

I turned my head, mostly to assure myself it was possible, rolled onto my knees, gathered what shreds of dignity I had left, and crawled back to my house.

Some days it would be better to just stay in bed.

Manure Capers

For several years cow manure and I spent a lot of time together.

Sounds like a bizarre statement, to say the least—and a revolting one—but I can assure you it's a fact.

And they were good years too!

Some time ago I secured a Class One drivers license—the same one big rig truckers must possess to ply their trade—since driving was always a thing I was reasonably good at.

Subsequently, it has afforded me an opportunity to drive some interesting vehicles, not the least of which was what we will now affectionately refer to as, the poop truck.

It all began when I responded to an advertisement seeking a driver for a local corral cleaning company.

On my first day at the job, I could see the owner, and doubtless the rest of the men, had some misgivings. Understandable, since the woman who showed up for work that morning sported an attractive outfit, spiffy hairdo and red lipstick. Hardly attire for the job at hand.

Need I remind you I was going to be working with cow manure, not women's fashion? However, they were all kind and put on brave faces as we motored out to the farmyard where the trucks were waiting.

I spent the first hour riding along with one of the seasoned veterans. Let's call him Lloyd.

Lloyd was pleasant company and thoroughly explained every move he made, what was expected of me, and any little quirks of the truck we were in.

It was important information since a lot could go wrong if improperly handled. Driving around on muck is not an easy task. It's much like trying to scoot across an ice rink in a lumber wagon.

After this time of instruction, it was my turn to maneuver the massive vehicle through an obstacle course of slippery trails and alleys before backing it up through a gate the size of a fridge door.

I wisely said nothing, but did as I was told and managed quite well, as it turned out.

Only one unlucky incident occurred to mar this otherwise satisfying time.

Prior to the close of each day there was a certain ritual of cleaning that took place.

At the back of these trucks is a huge auger which picks up the muck and flings it out across the land in a lovely measured spray. Inevitably, this auger catches a pile of twine from bales that have been left there, and winds the string tightly around itself. It's the driver's job to hack and rip away at this offending material with a sharpened knife to remove it.

What a miserable occupation it was!

For a start, I was in the precarious position of standing directly beneath the auger.

This meant, whatever the gunk on the unit happened to be, I could be assured it would rain down upon my unprotected head and face.

Some would dribble down my shirt where the warm heat of my body brought it to its full, ripened splendor.

Other, mushier hunks clung to clothing and dried, making me a fun person to hang out with in a confined space.

This was the unfortunate task I was employed in when my luck turned.

I've never been a person to swear. I find curses to be ugly in a world where there are so many other, fabulous choices at hand. As a consequence, all of my life I've had people remark with derision, "Aw that Helen. She wouldn't say s—t if her mouth was full of it." (You can probably tell where this is going.)

I labored at the back of the truck later that day, head thrown back, mouth gaping as I panted with exertion.

Sadly, due to my fevered slashing, a particularly large chunk of sloppy, wet muck flew gracefully up into the evening sky, performed a nimble arc in the air above my head before slapping into my opened mouth with horrifying accuracy!

I look back fondly on my poop truck days.

The men I worked with were a fine bunch of people and I miss our day-to-day banter, the farms we worked at and the laughs we shared.

I learned a lot about driving in difficult situations and ultimately discovered all those people were right in what they said: I really don't say s—t when my mouth is full of it.

Who Says Cows are Dull?

Are cattle merely large, docile animals lounging contentedly in fields across our great nation?

Do those who raise and care for them live out their days in comparative boredom and lackluster years of dullness?

Certainly not! And I'll prove it.

This incident took place a long time ago with my father and a veterinarian in our area, the late Dr. Glenn Weir.

Back then dad was establishing a herd of purebred Charolais cattle and each live calf was pretty important.

There were no fancy stock trailers in the 60s. For us, the only way to transport livestock was to run them up a chute and into the back of a truck fitted with stock racks. This was precarious at best. I remember hearing stories of animals that tried to spring over the top to freedom; a leap often ending in disaster.

On this particular day dad motored into town with a cow in need of a cesarean. She was forced, against her better judgment, into the small confines of his pickup, and she stomped suspiciously about with a wild look in her eyes.

Two large feet protruded from her hind end; the calf too large for dad to deal with.

However, giving birth was clearly secondary in the bovines mind as dad slowly backed up to the chute behind the clinic and she watched warily for a means of escape.

A couple of men appeared from the building. They stood, ready to guide the beast into the clinic as dad began lifting out the end gate.

One minute all was well, and the next dad was flat on his back in the gravel holding fragments of splintered wood as the cow lunged heavily over him and bolted off across the parking lot.

There were no houses behind the clinic, although it was situated right in the middle of town. Only a stubble field and a droopy wire fence, which the crazed bovine cleared with a single bound in her quest for liberty.

The young men and my father lustily gave chase and were able, with effort and a lot of panting, to bring her back around to the parking lot.

The wide back doors had been flung open and a gathering of roughly thirty men had assembled in a semi-circle to prevent her fleeing again.

Wild-eyed, she took one look at them, her eyes rolled back in her head, and she rushed, with renewed fortitude, right through the middle and out the other side scattering men like bowling pins in her wake.

With reckless abandon she galloped down the grassy

verge near the clinic and out onto the middle of the busy Yellowhead Highway.

Cars screeched to a halt, horns blared, curses rose upon the afternoon air and the large contingent of men turned of one accord and raced en masse across the highway after her.

There was a hotel across the road at that time, built in a U-shape. The agitated animal dashed into its parking lot and bolted toward the office with a loud clattering of hooves: her eyes wide and glaring, nostrils flared and sides heaving.

Glenn Weir, who had been watching these proceedings with great interest from the quiet repose of his clinic window, now saw a glorious opportunity for a laugh. Quickly dialing the number of the hotel office he calmly asked the girl behind the desk, "Do you have a room ready for Miss Bossy? She's waiting at the window." The woman screamed loud and long as she turned to behold the demented beast lurch to a halt inches from the glass.

It all ended well, however. Several of the men in pursuit thought to bring lassos and deftly caught the now exhausted cow.

With a few men pulling, and a few more pushing, they made their way once again across the highway, amid much fanfare from passing motorists and assorted onlookers, and into the clinic where a live calf was born.

Docile? Cattle? I think not!

Enough With the Cats Already!

While making no secret of the fact I'm a card-carrying member of the I Love Cats club, a line must be drawn somewhere.

Briefly I can tell you a stray showed up on our deck this past April, pregnant and abandoned.

We created a warm kennel for Coconut—so named for her creamy mottled fur—and she gave birth to four adorable kittens.

All was going well until the afternoon she disappeared. We searched for her in vain and it was concluded, with much sadness, she had fallen prey to a coyote.

In desperation we rang my father to see if he had any milk replacement (for calves) that we could hopefully feed to the kittens.

"You want milk for WHAT?" he asked incredulously. But that didn't work anyway since, who knew cats were lactose intolerant?

The kittens were barely two weeks old, so Aliyah started researching information on how to raise them. They were brought inside, and a frantic trip was made at 10 p.m. for supplies. Aliyah and I then sat cross-legged on the floor much of the night trying to force food down the tiny kittens' resistant little gullets.

And here's a further bit of news; kittens can't eliminate waste (I'm trying to be gentile here people) without stimulation from the mother on their hind ends.

This put us in the awkward position of massaging a cat's butt.

A lot.

The sentence, "Yay, he peed on my leg," was not one I'd ever imagined myself uttering, let alone being happy about.

Thankfully, late next day, Coconut returned. Or, to put it in other terms—we thought she was a goner, but the cat came back (sorry, it was too good to resist.)

Aliyah's room was turned into a cat den, Coconut was brought inside, and the saga continued. Fast-forward a few weeks and there are cats every bloody place you look. Six cats are too many for anyone I tell you!

My friend (and at this point I use the term loosely) Susan, has all along laughingly maintained I've acquired a "crazy cat lady starter kit".

Grudgingly, I may be forced to admit she's right since, as I write, one kitten scales the drapery, another tussles with his mother's tail and two more claw their way up the sofa.

Mouse, (yes, it is his name) our previous cat resident,

occasionally pins one down, despite shrill protest, and licks it thoroughly. Initially Aliyah was concerned Mouse was tasting the kitten's fur to see if it could become dinner but no, he was just giving it a good wash.

The other night I heard an insistent tapping on my bedroom door, "Mom, I need you," Aliyah hissed. I padded out into the living room where she grasped my shoulders and searched my face with a wild eye.

"A cat has pooped in my bed," she pronounced in despairing tones.

"Good to know," I yawned, turning sleepily away.

"No!" she leapt forward blocking my path, "You've gotta help me remove it. Well, to be honest, I'll wait outside while you do it," she finished truthfully.

My eyes narrowed and then I shrugged and shuffled off to fetch some tissue and clean sheets.

"It's under there," she declared moments later, pointing with a quavering finger to a spot on her bed. I peeled back the offending covers (with effort since they were sticky) and beheld a nasty, brown, flattened mass. Grasping it firmly with the paper towel, I began to peel it up.

"Ack!" Aliyah shrieked as a portion of the mound came away in my hand. "How revolting."

Strangely, the room began to take on the pleasing scent of spearmint and tentatively I brought the wad up to my nose for further inspection. "MOM, are you crazy?" Aliyah yelled in disgust from the doorway. I took a deep sniff and then turned to her night table where an empty box of treats lay discarded and forgotten.

Regarding her as she hovered anxiously by the door, I said, "Snacking under the covers again I presume? This isn't cat poop you little ninny, it's a melted mint patty.

All in all, the cat theme has been entertaining and at times a trifle overwhelming, but I'm not really complaining—kittens are so cute, and we'll find them homes.

There's only one significant problem at this point—a new cat is sitting on the deck peering through the window at me as we speak.

ENOUGH WITH THE CATS ALREADY!

Fire Hazards

At work last week, while happily boiling water to make a cup of cocoa, I was made keenly aware of the fire hazards involved in such an act.

Our Wellness Coordinator, Anne, employed at the same school where I work, had asked me to disconnect the kettle immediately after use, explaining how easily small appliances can combust.

Immediately I thought of the one I'd left plugged in at home. Yikes!

Of course, it wouldn't be my first kitchen fire.

Once, at the tender age of 12, I felt the need to eat a fried egg. (Fried eggs aren't usually the basis of a good story, but I'm going to give it a shot.)

It was winter, and for some reason I was at home alone, an oversight I'm sure my parents later regretted.

In those days, we fried food in bacon fat. There were no unpleasant repercussions to our health for such cooking methods, and no dire warnings of cholesterol or saturated fats that I recall. In any case, I scraped a pound of hardened grease into the fry pan and turned the element to high before settling myself in front of the television to watch an episode of The Flintstones.

Was an entire pound really necessary you ask? Should I have left a boiling vat of lard unattended, you inquire? Of course not, but I was 12 and a bit of a nut.

Soon, my attention was dragged away from Fred and Wilma by oily, black clouds of smoke that rolled lazily across the ceiling above me.

GOOD GRIEF!

I leapt from my chair to see a four-foot wall of hungry orange flames licking the kitchen ceiling. I raced to the stove trying to remember what Smokey the Bear had done in this situation, but couldn't recall Smokey ever frying eggs.

Wait! He'd cover the blaze!

I snatched a thin metal lid off the counter and threw it on the smoking pan. The lid promptly melted into a horrid, twisted puddle, but at least the fire was out.

Using a tea towel to shield my arm, I turned off the element. However, smoke still poured from the heated fat.

Lifting everything with the towel, I made to rush outside and pitch the whole mess into a snowdrift, but it was too hot. I was forced to set the pan down immediately—right onto the shiny new linoleum Dad recently applied to our kitchen floor. You can imagine how that turned out.

As you can see, I've had a nasty go-round with a kitchen appliance before. It was quite some time ago and it could be hoped I'd learned from my mistakes, but I have a crummy memory.

This Monday, while trundling along in the bus, I glanced up and noticed a smoky jet-trail in the sky.

RATS!

I'd forgotten the blasted appliances again.

Groaning, I envisioned a raging inferno engulfing my happy home; the fluffy faces of my three innocent cats pressed to the windows, pleading for release; all thanks to my selfish desire for a hot beverage.

Thank you Anne for opening my eyes to this folly. I shall never be the same happy-go-lucky, carefree woman again.

And now, if you'll excuse me, I have to get home to unplug the kettle.

Let Them Eat Cake

During the early years of farming on the prairies, home cooks didn't have the luxury of popping into the grocery store at a moment's notice.

They didn't own bread makers, mixers or high tech ovens. Nor did they possess a plethora of cookbooks, or watch television programs dedicated to the culinary arts.

They worked with limited ingredients, resources and equipment and made do with what they had.

Nonetheless, they fed their families wholesome, nutritious foods and all were better for a simpler diet.

I recall my grandmother relying on an old Blue Ribbon Cookbook for inspiration. The pages became splattered and worn from years of use, and eventually were only held together with the rubber ring off an old sealer jar.

Now, some 60 years later, that same book is a cherished antique; its lifetime of faithful service rewarded with a place of honor on my bookshelf.

One recipe for a spice cake stands out in my memory.

It featured raisins—boiled to within an inch of their plump, sticky little lives—and a sprinkling of cinnamon, nutmeg and cloves all stirred briskly into a stiff batter. Then it was skidded into the old wood stove to be baked.

The cake often turned a little black on top since the heat was difficult to regulate, but when it was sliced hot and placed steaming on the table before us, the aroma was heavenly.

Sadly, I hated it.

I can recall this miserable dessert only because I was forced to gum it down regardless of a deep loathing for the revolting fruit it contained.

Kids ate whatever food was put before them back then and felt, at least according to my father, "BLOODY LUCKY TO HAVE IT."

Another interesting volume I have on the shelf arrived on a ship from England with my grandparents.

This tome is a true relic of a bygone era. Among such award winning recipes were Soused Mackerel (had they spent all night swilling beer in a pub?) Stuffed Ox Cheek, Jugged Hare (yum) and Stewed Neck of Lamb.

A few ingredients, for a recipe by the somewhat off-putting name of Dough Cake, includes six ounces of good drippings, a little tepid milk and one teacup of golden syrup.

Tepid milk and syrup are understandable, but this teacup business is a bit strange. And what the heck are good drippings? Are they easily distinguishable from bad drippings or is that just the chance we take?

Furthermore, from where exactly did they drip? Inquiring minds want to know.

Time has passed and while I retain my raisin boycott, I've developed an unfortunate penchant for cake.

A long time ago, when I was first married, I wished to prove myself as an excellent cook.

One evening I busily baked up a moist and delicious carrot cake with extra creamy frosting. Next morning, I cut a large wedge of the delectable treat and popped it into hubby's lunch pail. After he left, I busied myself with small household chores, keeping an eye on aforementioned cake.

Finally, I allowed myself just one piece. After all, it was important to sample it for quality assurance, you understand.

Well, one thing led to another and over the course of the day I found myself hovering over the dish until all that remained were crumbs on the floor and icing on my upper lip. I had devoured the whole flaming thing! In my defense it was an 8x8 pan; not a triple layer monstrosity, but still, appalling behavior to say the least.

Ashamed of this dreadful deed, I paced the floor, staring at the clock. Soon my spouse would return after working hard in the elements all day. How could I possibly answer when he asked for dessert?

"What cake? Oh right, well the dog ate it," I answered offhandedly, to test its believability. It probably would have worked if we owned a dog.

Then I tried, "Good grief man! We've been robbed!" Nope, couldn't do it. Hurriedly I baked and iced another cake. With minutes to spare I hacked off the identical wedge, bolted it down and smiled a smile of felonious greed as he walked through the door.

This tale may have had more to do with purging my guilty conscience than a discussion of early country cake baking, but it shall remain as a warning for all who hope to keep baked goods safe in my presence.

Remember, the secret lies in raisins—and plenty of 'em.

Mouse Tales

After working for several arduous years in the field of education, I've finally earned a few letters behind my name. Unfortunately, they aren't the sort that prompt a raise in pay, or elicit respect from peers or faculty members. No, these letters actually spell out a rather unpleasant word: KILLER!

It all started Saturday when our three cats settled themselves in front of the dishwasher and maintained a silent surveillance throughout the afternoon. Naturally, I assumed a rodent had foolishly scuttled into our home, and was now lurking, with understandable fear and trembling, beneath this sturdy kitchen appliance.

I baited a trap, set it inside a nearby cupboard (so no cats would be snapped) and forgot about it.

In hindsight, I wouldn't necessarily advise people to "forget about" wayward vermin that invade their living space, but I did.

Later that evening, my grandson Kayden, who was over for a visit, along with my daughter Aliyah and I, lounged on the sofa watching a movie. Candles flickered moodily on a shelf over the television, the fire crackled and snapped in the next room, and we snuggled under blankets feeling warm and cozy, mesmerized by the height of the action.

Suddenly a low growling, deep in the chest of Nemo the

cat interrupted our involvement in the thickening plot. My girl glanced toward the source.

"He has a mouse!" she screeched, rearing up from her chair. As you can well imagine, complete pandemonium ensued.

Kayden leapt onto the couch and ran back and forth across it hollering, "Can I keep him?"

My daughter pranced from the room shrieking, "Don't kill it."

I raced for some sort of weapon groaning, "Holy crap." Nemo hissed between teeth clenched tightly round a squirming mouse, "He's mine you fools."

And last but not least, the mouse squeaked, "Somebody listen to that girl!"

With all the hollering and fuss, Nemo lost his bravado, his jaw went slack, and he dropped the mouse with a little thud to the carpeting. Picking itself up, the sodden rodent scampered dizzily across to the next cat in line that snatched him up and hunkered on the floor amid fresh yelling from the sofa and the dining room respectively.

"I could keep him in a cage," and "Please let him live," rang in my ears as I charged into the room brandishing a broom.

"EEK," I squealed in alarm, as the mouse was spat onto the floor once again, but as it scurried off I pulled myself together, briskly bonked it on the head with the dustpan, swept it up and carried it outside.

"YOU KILLED IT!" my girl shouted in shock and revulsion. Then, pointing a trembling finger, she pronounced dramatically, "Never again shall I set foot in this room where innocent blood was shed!"

"Cut the theatrics," I answered irritably, setting my instruments of death back in the closet. "What was I supposed to do? Fix him a light snack and offer him a lift into town? Blow-dry his fur and introduce him to a few friends over drinks? Buy him a condo in the city? He's a bloody mouse!"

In any event, the evening was over. Kayden trailed off to bed bemoaning his lost chance at a pet, Aliyah marched to her room in stiff disapproval, and I sit here alone—a cold-blooded killer.

Stuck On the Prairies

My friend Gwen recently documented an incident on Facebook in which she became stuck in a snowdrift trying to exit her yard. She snapped a lovely photo of the sunrise to commemorate the event, and later we discussed times we've each been in sticky situations.

For me, most of these occasions focus on manure, as troubles in life often do. During the years I worked driving a truck for Dave, at Bulldog Corral Cleaning, I found myself wedged into some unusual spots due to the stuff.

Once the tires of a truck get slicked up with cow crap, there isn't much a person can do to break free. Of course, it isn't always easy to avoid. The vehicle must be maneuvered in and out of corrals that are situated on hills, through narrow gates, alongside feed troughs or next to sheds, all while traversing the exceedingly slippery substance. Each farm held a plethora of challenges and I experienced my fair share of them all. Nonetheless, it wasn't me who ended up stuck in this particular story.

It was on a day when our fleet of trucks were parked, waiting for us, at a farmyard built along the banks of Saskatchewan's Battle River. As often happened, we had a new driver starting work that morning.

The fellow was no stranger to trucks, having driven them much of his life, but he was a loudmouth of the most irritating kind. Bumping along in the three-quarter ton that morning, we'd all been treated to his opinion and expertise on innumerable subjects.

Then, to culminate the miserable trip, he'd actually asked me if my reason for "tagging along" that day was to provide lunch for the men. Idiot!

The other occupants of the vehicle fell uncomfortably silent as I spun in my seat with a frown and tuned him in.

Later, as we readied the trucks, Dave issued a few instructions before mopping his brow and clanking off across the yard in the CAT.

It appeared easy enough to back through the gate and up to where he waited near the shed, but it was deceptively tricky. I don't remember his name, but Johnny Know-it-all (as I dubbed him) laughed derisively as he swaggered toward his vehicle.

With a dismissive glance toward me, he flicked a cigarette from his mouth and said, "I'll go first and show the little lady how it's done."

He was overflowing with confidence, I'll give him that. However, not too bright, since if there's one sure way to aggravate a woman it's to condescendingly call her the little lady. I stood silently by to watch the scene unfold.

Dave's CAT was perched on a crest at the far end of the corral with a brimming bucket of slop held high in the air. It was our job to back under that bucket perfectly so all he would have to do is dump it.

There was only one possible angle to enter the gate, which meant turning the wheel at just the right moment to climb the knoll and maintain momentum. Conversely, too much momentum could send us sliding over the other side.

It was a long way down to where the river gurgled below. Also, it's pretty near impossible to drive straight up a mound of muck let alone back up it.

It would be necessary to get on this hill at the low end where there was a bit of dry ground and then back along it lengthwise.

Johnny Know-it-all rumbled off across the yard, ignoring earlier directives as he steered through the opening and attempted to power directly up to the peak.

Naturally, he knew best.

From a distance I saw Dave's eyes widen at this sudden insanity, and then his mouth open in a soundless torrent of profanity as the truck came to a squelchy halt and began sliding back down. Surprisingly, Johnny was able to pull out, but then tried again on the very same track that hadn't worked the first time!

He finished up in a swamp, sunk to the axles in deep muck and needing a tow.

Once Johnny was clear of the area, Dave hollered over the radio. "Helen, you get in here just the way I told you.

Show this joker some real drivin'!"

Without a word I pulled forward enough to give myself space to take a run at it. Releasing the clutch I roared confidently through, swung the truck around, turned it to find the dirt and kept the huge vehicle on the ridge till I pulled slowly in beside the CAT.

My employer said nothing further as he busily got to work, but peering out my window I could see him grinning broadly. He was pleased.

Getting stuck in snow, mud, or manure is all part of life on the prairies, but it was a poor start to Johnny's first day.

He sulked much of the afternoon and didn't stay with us very long after. As you can well imagine, everyone was really sorry to see him go—particularly the little lady.

Shut Up and Do It!

When the countryside starts to dry up in spring, and cattle are moved out of their wet, sloppy pens into a pasture of new, green grass, I always reflect back upon my days driving a truck.

As soon as possible we were hard at work from dawn till dusk and traveling from farm to farm to clear barnyards and fertilize fields. It was, perhaps, an unusual sort of job for a woman; particularly one who didn't leave the house each day without lipstick and earrings, but I liked it, and have fond memories—mostly.

People often asked me how I could work at such an occupation; spending each day motoring about the land in a truck filled with steaming piles of muck. However, it was nothing for a girl who grew up with manure on her boots and a Charolais cow in her heart (the cow part is a little overstated, but it'll make Dad happy).

Dave Wasyliw, the man who owned and ran the company, took pride in a job well done, and insisted on a high level of service for his customers. He was pretty particular as to how we handled the trucks, too, since foolish mistakes could be dangerous as well as costly.

Dave was good at what he did, and earned our respect. I learned to back a tandem truck into places you'd think twice about pushing a wheelbarrow through, while each day presented a challenge I grew to enjoy.

The men I toiled alongside were a jovial group and there was a lot of fun poked at the new woman on the job.

Nonetheless, I proved myself equal to the task, and was accepted without question until one cold day shortly after I started.

Our wheels crunched through a fresh skiff of snow as we rolled into a farmyard built up the side and over the top of a hill.

We helped Dave unload the CAT, and he trundled off toward the corrals to determine the best means of attack.

Driving a vehicle on cow manure is a slippery business, but when you add in a steep slope and four inches of snow there's bound to be trouble.

Finally, Dave's confident voice boomed over our truck radios.

"OK people, I want you to back through the gate at the bottom of the first corral facing east. Make sure you get up some speed so you make it up the hill and don't slide and crash into that shed at the bottom. Aim toward the gate at the top on a 45 degree angle, but before you reach it you've got to turn toward the south to get through. And be damned careful because it's narrow and I don't want any scraped up trucks!"

He took a breath and continued, "You can't stop up there

to make the turn so you've got to do it while you're moving. You won't get a second chance, so make it good. Once you're there, back down the passageway about 50 feet and through another gate that's even narrower. Gear down before it and watch your speed because it's straight downhill and there's a helluva drop on the left. There's another sharp turn at the bottom where I'll be waiting so get a move on."

"Oh yeah, and DON'T GET STUCK," he finished grimly.

I slumped in my truck, gripping the wheel with whitened knuckles.

What did he say? Surely I must have heard wrong. I went over it all again in my mind, every miserable detail etching itself into my brain.

The man made this obstacle course sound like a bloody stroll in the park!

I watched as the first truck roared off at the prescribed angle and disappeared behind weathered gray slabs. It flew up the grade, motor revving; fighting against the deep slop, which pulled it inexorably towards a shed hunching in a cesspool at the bottom.

Finally reaching the summit it turned abruptly and shot through the next gate.

"SLOW DOWN!" Dave yelled in agitation.

All too soon it was my turn. With clammy hands I

backed up to the starting point and surveyed the mountain of sludge behind me. One truck had already been dragged from its final resting place in the pit of despair; after it had slid sideways down the slope, barely missing the shed.

Now it was my turn. Peachy. This was where I made my critical error.

Before thinking of the consequences, I snatched up the radio and shrieked, "You have GOT to be kidding. This is impossible."

There was silence for a few moments and then the taunting remarks began. I took a lot of guff over my hasty words—for days. Turns out it wasn't actually impossible, and I successfully roared through it repeatedly over the next few hours.

Ultimately, this experience taught me not to flaunt my weaknesses lest I be ridiculed without end.

More than that, it imparted a valuable life lesson since now, when difficult situations present themselves, as they always do, I think of it, grit my teeth, hold my head high, shut up—and do it. Thanks Dave, you were a good man.

Wild Encounters?

I'm sure each of us could tell of a time when a close encounter with some wild animal took place.

Some could even speak of an instance where life and limb were threatened. Often we see news headlines from the Rocky Mountains where people dangerously meet up with grizzlies, or bull elk, but luckily we don't have to contend with them here.

While people in our area occasionally run across a black bear, it's still a rarity, and although cougars have been sighted nearby, they are far and few between. Nope, here on the prairies our wild encounters aren't usually hazardous unless we hit a moose on the highway.

As is often the case, I have a couple of accounts to share with you along this theme. These tales couldn't be measured as unsafe nor life threatening; they're more unhygienic and nasty than anything; revolting even. The first one begins on a visit to see a friend years ago. I'd arrived at midnight to her home in the country, and there was only time for a few hurried greetings before we bustled off to bed.

Yawning, I swiftly changed and tumbled in. I'd been driving much of the day with three small children clamoring, "Are we there yet?" and it was good to stretch out and relax. Granted, there appeared to be areas of some crumbly grit under the covers, but no matter—I dropped off to sleep.

Next morning I awoke as sunlight crept in through shutters I'd forgotten to close, causing me to squint blearily over the comforter and into the beady little eyes of a small, gray mouse.

"AHHHH!"

I screamed, flinging the covers away and launching myself perpendicular to the wall.

"AHHHH!" screeched the mouse as it flew, flipped by the blanket to plummet through the air into a far corner of the room. I cannot presume to enter the mind of a mouse or speak on his behalf, but it seems pretty easy to play out the preceding events from his perspective.

Here he was, a mouse of the world with places to go and things to do; minding his own business after a hard night rummaging for crumbs on the kitchen floor.

Having found this place of quiet repose in the attic, he'd quietly retired to his hidden haven between the sheets of a comfortable bed only to find there was a hulking big intruder lying in wait. Noiselessly he'd crept to the edge of this soft home to scope out the scene and then had been murderously flung against a wall for his trouble.

I, on the other hand, shuddered convulsively for the next week thinking how I'd spent the night slumbering peacefully in the excrement of a mouse.

Another incident also occurred on a visit, but this time with my Uncle Don and Aunt Esther.

Again, I'd arrived the evening before and we'd visited happily before turning in for the night. I'd arisen early, before anyone else, and enjoyed sluicing my face with a refreshing splash of water, leisurely brushing my teeth, and bathing luxuriously in a hot, deep tub full of water. With a sigh of contentment, I reclined back into the sudsy liquid, until my uncle interrupted my morning ablutions, and spoke tersely through the bathroom door.

"I hope you haven't used the water yet, Helen?" he asked anxiously. "I forgot to tell you we found a dead mink floating in the cistern last night."

"WHAT?" I hollered, rearing up from the steamy depths.

I emerged moments later in a hastily knotted bathrobe to see my uncle peering sorrowfully through a trap door built into the floor. I knelt to join him.

Yes, there it was, bloated, black and shapeless; riding the ripples of my recent water consumption.

Wasn't that just my bloody luck! I'd never get to see a mink in the wild, oh no. My introduction to the elusive creature was to view it drifting face down in my drinking water.

Three cheers for an active immune system too, since as you will notice, I didn't in fact die from this event.

Needless to say, these accounts can't honestly compete with stories of real animal confrontations. I mean, who hasn't dealt with a mouse at one time or another? Of course, perhaps you haven't locked eyes with the rodent three inches from your nose while recumbent in bed, but still. And although running into a live mink might qualify, bathing in juices rendered from his watery tomb fails to make the grade on any scale.

Clearly I shall have to do better in my quest for true wild animal encounters. Sorry.

An Apple a Day...

Home remedies, popular before we had access to the doctors and medicines we do today, have made quite a comeback.

Way back when, people used whatever cures they had at hand; tried and true tonics and strange mixtures handed down from the trusted hands of great-grandma.

Were they really so bad? Perhaps a few of them are still worth considering. Others could cheerfully be tossed out the back door.

Here's a small admission before we begin—the only real vice I've ever had was salt. There, I've said it and you may quote me, my name is Helen and I am a salt-aholic.

However, in my defense, salt not only flavors our food, but can be dissolved in warm water and gargled as an old-fashioned remedy for a sore throat, or swished orally as an aid to healing nasty cold sores.

Of course, there's a certain amount of stinging associated with that last one, but as my mother always said, with a dismissive wave of her hand, "Quit your bloody moaning. It's doing you some good."

Caution though: Do not ingest! If taken internally, this concoction may cause an unexpected evacuation of your bowels.

Speaking of bowels, and at the risk of becoming too earthy for my readership, generations of mothers and grandmothers advocated the consumption of stewed prunes for constipation. I know I had a few of them forced down my young gullet back in the day. Can't say I was ever too thrilled at the prospect of slurping down the brown, sticky lumps, but there is something to it. They're a natural source of fiber, and along with plenty of water can be counted on to "do the trick," so to speak. Alternately, my grandmother would boil a pot of milk for the opposite problem and could be counted on to deal it out lavishly.

"That'll stop you up Helen," she'd say with a grim smile, settling a mug of steaming milk on the table in front of my startled eyes. She'd fold her arms across an ample bosom and wait for me to drain the cup before patting my shoulder with satisfaction.

Unfortunately, a disagreeable skin always seemed to form quickly over the surface.

Boiled milk—bleah.

What about slowly sucking on a teaspoon of honey for coughs?

That was one I didn't mind as a kid. I've even been known to dispense the odd spoon of it to my own children. In theory, it's supposed to sooth and lubricate the throat. Not sure that it does mind you, but it makes for quite a tasty treat and cuts down on whining by 50 per cent.

Here's one you may not have heard of; apple juice to

ward off the common cold. Frankly, I think it was a belief held exclusively by my mother. If ever brother Bill or I would make the dreadful mistake of coughing, mom's head would snap up and she'd bark, "You kids get a cup and pour yourselves a big glass of apple juice—or twenty."

My goodness, we couldn't even clear our throats or choke on a crumb without fearing her heavy-handed plying of the juice can. Curse you SunRype!

Of course, who can forget having your chest briskly rubbed with Rawleigh's medicated ointment to break up congestion? Or was I the only one who endured its liberal application?

Sorry Mr. Rawleigh, in actual fact your ointment wasn't the problem. The problem was the flippin' wool sock pinned round our necks to somehow amplify its benefits.

Who the heck came up with that evil instrument of torture?

"Now let's see, how can we keep that liniment from rubbing off on your shirt little Jimmy? Oh I know, let's wrap your tender young skin with this abrasive, unbearably scratchy, old woolen sock your father hauled off his foot late last night. Now, just hold still while I fasten it over your heart with this three-inch safety pin." Crazy people!

My final memory is of a small measure of hard liquor administered to me by my beloved father. In his all-seeing wisdom he recalled, from somewhere in his strict English upbringing, this unusual remedy for indigestion.

Perhaps it held curative powers highly favored by WWII British Naval officers, but it wasn't very effective for small girls with tummy aches.

He splashed a small amount of the amber liquid carefully into a tumbler and handed it over with full confidence in my speedy recovery. Are you kidding me? I was never so bloody sick in all my life.

In any case, despite my mockery, I do have faith in some natural remedies. It's certainly beneficial if we can avoid chemicals or harsh treatments in favor of gentler ones.

Just keep away from me with your juice, hallucinogenics and old socks.

I'd rather be sick.

Dear Abby (Helen)

I'm sure, at some point in your life, you've had the chance to speak a few words of encouragement or wisdom into someone's life.

It can be life changing for both parties. Such openings come each and every day when you work with children.

It's a responsibility never taken lightly by those who are in education, at least by the teachers I know. Even something as simple as a smile or nod can bring reassurance to a small worried face, and a few genuine, caring words can mean all the difference in a child's day.

Of course kids aren't the only ones who benefit from kindness and positive reinforcement. Words are powerful tools. I'm sure we can all think of someone who made an impression in our lives with something supportive they said along the way.

Shortly before the following incident took place I attended an information evening at our local high school with my daughter.

Kids entering high school are encouraged to think seriously about their future, and carefully make the important decisions that ultimately shape it. Teachers instruct not only math and language arts, etc., but they help prepare each child to face the world as they make these first steps towards independence and autonomy.

It was with all of this in mind that, some days later, I responded to a small, persistent voice several seats back on my bus. Up to this point the most pressing issue at hand had been avoiding potholes on a bumpy grid road, but now this: "Mrs. Toews, Johnny is scared he might grow up."

I gathered myself with a start; this was a significant moment!

My mind raced for the right words to hearten this youngster who was clearly concerned about leaving his childhood behind. I glanced back in my mirror. His eyes opened wide with unspoken fear and a lower lip that trembled ever so slightly.

Good grief, this child was looking to me for some strong message of cheer; some advice, which would carry him through the next few years with a glad heart and renewed purpose. OK—so he's only eight years old—what of it!

He still looked as though the weight of the world was on his shoulders. I pulled into the next yard, stopped the bus and opened the door for the next passenger.

Shuffling his feet into the aisle, he inched forward on his seat and stared down the aisle at me with mute appeal in his glistening eyes. Help, they seemed to say. I began to utter words of reassurance and promise for his success in life. I outlined at some length his bright prospects and the assurance of great destiny.

Warming to my subject I raised a finger above my head and shook it with conviction as I expanded on this worthy theme. The boy smiled wanly, and then leaned a suddenly ashen face upon the seat in front of him and I saw his lips moving as he whispered some further instruction to the original spokesman.

Wow, I thought with a swell of pride, I'm really getting through to this kid. I opened my mouth to deliver a confident closing remark when the spokesman interrupted loudly, "Stop Mrs. Toews, you've got it all wrong! Bobby didn't say he was scared about growing up. He said he was scared he might THROW UP."

Needless to say I clapped my mouth shut and attended to the poor child's needs immediately. He hadn't required an orator; just a bit of fresh air and a bucket.

I guess I should add to my earlier statement: one must also be sensitive to the needs of others before delivering unsolicited advice.

Lessons Learned

I come from a family of great penny-pincher's. My parents taught me well. Of course, we prefer to think of ourselves as thrifty, economical or even cautious, but it all boils down to the same thing—CHEAP.

I think it comes from having parents and grandparents who lived through the dirty '30s and other tough times. They knew how to re-purpose long before it became trendy. Syrup tins became lunch pails, hand-me-downs were expected and there was zero waste. It was a way of life.

When I was a kid I didn't understand all that.

Once, after visiting the home of a young friend, I whined to my mother, "Deborah has so many pretty dresses. Why don't I?"

In a fresh wave of misery, I recalled a recent Christmas concert where I'd dreamed of sweeping through the door in a white lace dress with pink satin sash, as advertised in Eaton's Winter Catalogue. Instead, I stalked stiffly to my seat wearing an inflexible red pantsuit made for a kid half my height and twice my girth.

Thank you bargain bin.

With a sigh mom patted my hand, "You have something better than pretty dresses." Her voice lowered to become conspiratorial and dramatic, "You have a little brother."

What? Are you kidding me? I glanced up to see my brother Billy spin through the kitchen on a small red tricycle.

Bent low over the handlebars, he pedaled furiously, rounded the corner and as something dragging behind him hit the door jamb with a smack, he paused to cast a triumphant sneer in my direction. It was one of my favorite dolls with a length of binder twine tied roughly about her neck.

"Ask her if she wants him," I growled, turning back to my mother. "I'll trade her for the dresses."

A few years later, I became nearsighted. Thus began the era of "serviceable glasses". A visit to our optometrist for new spectacles did not include gazing into a mirror to assess the attractiveness of new styles. We didn't consider the shape of my face or the beautifying effects of flower detailing or colorful plastic. My father waved his arm with grim finality when I pleaded, and sternly addressed the woman helping us.

"I want something strong and serviceable for this girl. I want glasses that LAST," he pronounced loudly.

"How about those?" He pointed to some heavy wire frames in an aviator style popular among men preparing for a stint in the Canadian Air Force (or so I felt).

"Nooo," I moaned, but it was pointless to argue. The

silver goggles were strapped to my head and dad beamed with pleasure.

Another catch phrase at our house was, "Buy clothes big. She'll grow into 'em." This is all fine and dandy when purchasing items for children, but not so great when you're 16 and are presented with a puffy, green feather jacket from the menswear department of the Army and Navy Surplus store.

I didn't want to bloody GROW into it. It was huge! Does anyone, particularly during their formative teens, ever choose to resemble the Hunchback of Notre Dame, or wish to plod through school dressed as a Loggerhead Sea Turtle?

Anyway, as stated, I've learned these lessons well, and now, if you'll excuse me, I must speak to my daughter. "Aliyah, come here and try this coat I bought on sale yesterday.

"Sure, it's too big now—but you'll grow into it."

Never Enough Time

When you earn your living from the land it seems there are never enough hours in a day do all that needs doing.

There are animals to care for, crops to plant and tend, buildings to maintain, fences to fix and machinery that needs constant attention.

Lo and behold you get a good stretch of warm weather, hurry to the field with a smirk on your face while thinking how you've finally got a jump on things, and something breaks down.

By the time you get it fixed and pull out of the yard again, it starts to rain. How frustrating!

I remember years ago when my father complained bitterly about Daylight Savings Time; specifically the leap forward in spring. This disruption in his daily routine and the loss of one perfectly good hour was a source of great annoyance to him. One year he flatly refused to comply. Griping loudly about losing much needed sleep, he stood glaring up at the clock on our kitchen wall. The rest of the family accepted his refusal with minimal eye rolling, but it soon posed a significant problem.

My brother and I were still in school, mom held a part-time job in Lloydminster and we had various events to attend.

"Alright Les," my mother said in exasperation as she prepared school lunches early one morning, "You have to get the kids to school for nine, which is eight to you, and then you say you'll be feeding the cattle till noon. But is that your noon or mine? Lunch congealed on the stove for an hour yesterday waiting for you."

She paused and dad purposefully made for the door, head down, eyes averted. Mom fell into step right behind him. "Oh, and don't forget we have a concert in town tonight at the hall. We need to be there at seven which of course is six to you so you'd better be in to clean up by four thirty your time because if you show up at five like you did last week, that's six to us and we'll have missed the whole bloody thing."

She drew a long exaggerated breath, eyeing him darkly as she waved a peanut butter sandwich at his retreating back.

Needless to say, this schedule couldn't be maintained over the long haul and quickly passed into historic memoirs later referenced under the title, "A Season of Trouble".

Time is also a problem as we age.

Days and years slip by all too quickly and suddenly one day we're told our high school graduating class is gathering for a 40th reunion. I'm not suggesting this event is in any way linked to me, but FORTY! How can it possibly be? At times like this, human nature leads us to reflect back on all we meant to achieve, if only we had made the time. Often, we dwell too long in the negative, where regrets can overwhelm us.

My greatest aspiration in life was to be a writer. It's documented clearly in the LCHS yearbook alongside my spotty visage and frizzy hair. I can honestly say, while I enjoy my job very much, I did not, as a teenager, lie awake nights dreaming of becoming a bus driver.

Also, returning as an EA to the elementary school I once frequented as a child didn't figure even remotely into future plans I'd mapped out.

In fact, as I shook the dust from my feet on the last day of grade nine, I recall vowing never to return. Nonetheless, we play the hand we're dealt and I'm happy.

Is there some point to all this whining you may ask? Why yes, I believe there is. I have a wondrous solution for us all, handed to me many years ago by a dear man named Dugald McTavish. I unearthed it recently from a dusty cardboard box where it had been forgotten. (No wonder I've fallen so far behind!) Now I've found it again I expect to get much more accomplished.

It's simply this—a Round Tuit. This particular Round Tuit comes in the form of a small circular plaque, which is easily transportable and may be applied to any time constrained situation you find yourself in.

It's rare, mind you. I've only ever seen one, but I'm sure you could locate one if you looked hard enough.

In every situation where you find yourself saying, "I'd

have finished that project long ago if I could get around to it," or "This job needs doing, but I just can't get around to it," you now have no excuse.

Think of the possibilities!

If you acquired your very own round tuit; a lack of time would never plague you again.

Henceforth, I shall carry mine with me everywhere. What an invention.

A Sporting Event

Playing ball is a big part of early summer entertainment for many folks on the prairies. To spend an afternoon watching the game with hot-dog in hand, or to personally participate in the sport can be great for relaxing, exercising or meeting new people; even if you're not the sporty type. Despite limited involvement in this activity, I searched back into the annals of time and came up with one thematic tale to share.

Here goes: Many years ago, when I was young and reasonably fit, I joined a softball team that promoted themselves as playing purely for enjoyment. In fact, it appeared all fun and games on the surface, but beneath each low-brimmed ball cap lurked a dark desire to be at the TOP of the league! They yearned to clutch the shiny plastic trophy at season end, and some stopped at nothing to win the tawdry golden prize.

As for my team, it was soon understood I was no great player and I found myself dispatched far into left field. It was a pleasant place. Mostly I watched ants go about their business or imagined what was being served for supper in the houses nearby. Until one fateful day.

We'd all arrived at the ball diamond in good spirits and mingled with the opposing team before getting underway. Suddenly, I recognized an old classmate among the crowd; a tall strapping fellow with burly arms and a sneering face.

He spotted me too and nodded curtly in my direction. "Crud," I muttered under my breath. This pompous fellow had asked me on a date during high school, but I'd refused him, citing a life-threatening heart disorder and broken leg. I had neither, and he knew it. It hadn't gone well.

The game progressed without incident until we were up by one run in the seventh inning. The other team wasn't happy, and sneering guy was getting mad. "Hey Helen," he shouted, as I came up to bat, "How's your heart? Looks like it's a problem today, because you can't hit a damn thing."

Continuing, he jeered, "Maybe you should break another leg; it'd be less embarrassing than playing like crap."

Needless to say, I struck out and trailed sadly off to my usual position, questioning my presence on the team. Then sneery guy moved in to bat with bases loaded.

As the ball crossed home plate he wound up and walloped it high, high, high in the air—straight at me. ACK! My team hollered and screamed. His team hollered and screamed, but above the din his powerful voice could be heard bawling, "Run! She can't catch!"

Was I going to fumble? Would I flub it up? Was it my destiny to join Charlie Brown as the perpetual goat? I squinted into the sun and capered across the grass with vain hopes of catching the bloody thing.

Down it plummeted from the clouds (or thereabouts) and dashing forward I lunged into the air, thrusting my glove up, up into the sky.

Unbelievably, it bounced in.

I grabbed it, the umpire hollered, "You're out!" and I experienced the one and only triumph of my short, un-athletic career.

In conclusion, the moral of this story could well be about sportsmanship, fair play or team spirit, but actually is as follows: if you lie to an arrogant idiot it may come back to haunt you. Just saying.

Absolutely Shocking

This past spring, as always, farmers busily tilled, seeded and tended the land. Then they watch and wait as their fields take on lush shades of green and fill out with the promise of a bountiful yield.

During harvest last year, most farmers were already beginning to calculate what crops would be sown the next season. After careful consideration, they chose from the many seed options available, much the same as when we select from all possible varieties for the garden.

My garden, such as it is, grows steadily among the weeds. I always admire people with thriving, productive gardens. It's on my bucket list to grow one before I die, but sadly the item most likely to go with me to the grave unfulfilled.

Sigh. My loving son Chris was over last fall for a visit with his children, and peered thoughtfully out the kitchen window at my flourishing vegetable plot.

"You gonna bale that?" he asked, giving a backward smirk toward his mother.

After dealing out a well-deserved blow for insubordination, I stood beside him to gaze at the mass of tall, tangled quack grass and assorted thistles, rustling in the afternoon breeze.

He was right; it could be baled. I hate when he's right.

A few years ago, I resolved to make my dream true.

I set aside time each evening to spend on my hands and knees praying for help—wait, no—I meant to say, pulling weeds. Remarkably, by the end of July I almost had the place looking like a snapshot from Butchart Gardens. Diligence was really paying off until I lost ground one muggy day when hubby Tom decided to let the horses onto the lawn to, "graze it down a little."

Carefully he strung electric fence just inside the garden perimeter and assured me he would only let them into the area under strict supervision.

Spluttering with indignation at this clomping great intrusion, I crept beside a row of green beans, angrily plucking stink-weed from the soil and tossing it in a heap.

Slowly I worked my way to the south end. A gentle rain had begun to fall and I glanced up to push hair from my eyes and glare at the huge creatures tearing at grass three feet away. That move, a sizzling sound and the smell of burning hair were the last things I could remember when I woke up some time later face down in the radishes.

I'd forgotten the damnable fence! Crawling weakly from the flattened vegetation, I lay on the lawn to recover and comforted myself by imagining the various forms of revenge I could exact upon my beloved.

However, that would require energy and wits. Having

recently been electrocuted, I had neither.

At this time of year it certainly does a heart good to know another growing season is upon us. As for my dream, Butchart Gardens may be a nice place to visit, but I'll be content with a little fresh produce and less threat of electric shock therapy.

No horses allowed!

Age Is Only a Number

Sometimes milestone birthdays can get a person down. I have one approaching in the distance and who needs it?

I choose to be 38 and am sticking to it.

Here's what happened to remind me.

Early last Saturday morning I pulled up to a red light in a nearby town. Bright, warm sunshine flooded my older SUV. ABBA tunes blared and, singing along, I effortlessly slipped back to the 1980s.

It was going to be a fine day and I smiled into the rear-view mirror as a car approached from behind. At the last moment, the sleek, black sports car swerved into the next lane and purred up beside me.

Although I couldn't see the driver, I soon realized this person was watching for the light to change so they could take me off the line. The car surged forward once, then twice; its motor revving impressively each time, and I had a small flashback to my misspent youth. Back then my nickname was, oddly enough, Wheels.

I did a certain amount of racing in those days (sorry dad) and was hard to beat off a starting line. However, all this was long ago. Was I really prepared to charge across a deserted intersection in the middle of Vegreville at 7a.m., in some ABBA induced effort to relive old glory days?

HECK YEAH! After all, who did this nut think he was dealing with?

Thankfully, this inappropriate decision was taken out of my hands as the light quickly changed and the car shot away with a squeal of tires and the choking smell of burning rubber!

"Holy doodle," I said irritably, pulling alongside the now slowing vehicle.

Twisting my head, I peered through the window. What the heck? A white-haired, wizened old man of about 93 hunkered in the driver's seat (likely on a crocheted cushion).

He gripped the steering wheel with both hands and strained to see over his arthritic knuckles, but by golly, he could drive.

Feeling a rush of admiration for this fellow, I fell back in my seat to consider the whole event.

Either I've slipped badly and should consider throwing in the keys, or this guy has remarkable skill for his age. (Alternately, his foot may simply have slipped off the brake, but no matter, I'm sure it was the former).

Here's the deal—I want to be like him someday! Well, not exactly like him—thanks to a close relationship between myself and Miss Clairol, I don't plan on sporting white hair anytime soon, and the whole wizening thing can just pass me right on by, but clearly this man has sharp reflexes and an enviable talent that I admire.

So, the lesson to be gleaned here is as follows: don't get bogged down with worry over your age. It doesn't determine either your competence or ability in any arena of life. It's only a number after all. Choose one that represents you and hang on.

I like 38.

Beach Bums

Folks flocked to the beach this summer to bask in the sun and frolic in the waves.

Of course, a lake can offer many activities beyond these. It's a place to get away from it all, kick off your sandals, slap on the shades and RE-LAX. It's somewhere fishermen tirelessly cast their lines, boats scud across the azure water and countless sticky s'mores are slapped together and gobbled down amid laughter and fun. It's a spot to contemplate the stars, or perhaps our very existence as we recline in the warm sand, listening to gently lapping waves.

At least that's what I've heard. I'm not an authority since I never go, but it sounds good in theory. My fear of water is a serious hindrance to spending much time at lake's edge, and I don't even like crossing bridges, let alone crouching in a boat. I do in fact own a bathing suit, but haven't strapped it on in fifteen years, ever since brother Bill pointed out I looked like a black lab frantically paddling for shore. Couple this with several other unpleasant situations I've encountered, and it's no wonder I think twice before going.

When my son Chris was a young, impressionable lad, he and I took a trip to Victoria, B.C. to visit friends.

One sunny day we prepared a picnic lunch and spent time on a beach overlooking the Strait of Juan de Fuca. After picking our way along a shadowy trail, we climbed down a long flight of stairs and emerged on the sand below. The sun sparkled on waves that crested in the distance.

The tide was out and people were scattered everywhere searching for sand dollars, tiny crabs and shells. We rolled up our jeans, took off our shoes and did the same; passing several blissful hours before wandering down the coastline to find a quiet spot to dine.

The crowd had thinned behind us, but there appeared to be a large group some distance ahead. As we drew nearer Chris placed a hand on my shoulder and quietly spoke. "Mom, I think those people up there are naked."

"What?" I scoffed, "They can't be. This is a public area. They must be wearing flesh colored swim suits."

"All of them?" questioned my boy, squinting at me in disbelief.

Just in case, we stopped where we were and found a secluded spot among the rocks to contentedly munch a sandwich. Presently a man trudged past, carrying a guitar.

Chris poked me and hissed, "See. Nude!"

Granted the man was shirtless and pant-less, but undoubtedly he wore shorts. They were just hidden behind the instrument I assured my son with a smile.

Finishing up, we packed our things and headed back to the car. Along the way, loud, tuneless strumming jarred our senses and we turned toward the sound at the same horrible moment. Yes, there was the man. He sprawled unpleasantly over a nearby boulder, cradling the guitar close to his hairy chest—naked as a jaybird.

So yeah, beaches aren't my favorite place to go, but I'm sure the rest of you will have a great time.

Oh, and for future reference, very few people ever wear flesh-colored swim suits—and whole groups of them—probably never.

Just so you know.

Appearance vs Reality

Phaedrus, a Roman poet born in 15 BC, once said, "Things are not always as they seem; the first appearance deceives many."

It's a true statement on many levels. In real life it comes to play in how we perceive or judge others, how we evaluate relationships and circumstances, or even how we view the possibility of an afterlife.

We must realize everything we see and interpret is filtered through our own belief and opinion, and what we perceive to be truth about someone or something, may in fact, be the opposite.

This theme is also used with great effect in literature. Many of William Shakespeare's plays were written using this device, as The Bard toyed with the perceptions of his audience. But, interesting as this may be on an intellectual level, let's leave the deep theorizing behind for a moment since dry information was never my shtick. Suffice to say we should never judge something or someone's worth by their outward show.

I shall relay to you a short anecdote exemplifying the subject at hand. It opens on a warm summer day as my young children and I rumbled off to town in Ole Blue, our aged truck. We always watched for wildlife in those days—each of us for different reasons I didn't fully understand back then.

Becky and I kept our eyes peeled for the sake of innocent enjoyment, Justin scanned the landscape in order to win points for the animal game we always played, and Chris peered craftily out the window mentally sighting each happy woodland creature down the barrel of a gun. I suppose the barely audible, "Bang, bang," issued from his compressed lips ought to have been a giveaway, but I was just glad everyone was reasonably quiet for a blessed minute.

Anyway, each of us was absorbed in these uncomplicated pastimes as we rounded a sharp bend and saw—could it be—a bald eagle! This was at least 20 years ago and sightings of the majestic bird were less common than they seem to be now. We were thrilled.

Thankfully it was a quiet country road. I threw the truck into neutral, and we all strained forward on the seat as the motor was silenced and we began to coast.

"Get the camera," I hissed at Chris who sat near the glove compartment. He rummaged hurriedly in the dark depths before dragging it triumphantly forth.

Excitement in the truck was palpable as we slowly bore down upon the fabulous fowl. I imagined the tale we'd later tell of its massive white head, hooked beak and narrowed eyes. We would watch it peer down at us mere earthlings from its lofty perch and remark at the pleasure of this uncommon sight.

The immense bird sat in regal repose, preening its feathers atop a power pole—or so it appeared.

Did you catch the key word?

As we drew closer it seemed as though the bird began to struggle with some sort of inner turmoil. It lifted one leg to its head, then the other, and hopped ever so slightly into the air, spreading enormous wings. Chris lifted the camera to his eye and we all drew a sharp intake of breath as we watched the creature prepare for flight.

Crouching slightly, it gathered itself and took a mighty leap skyward as Becky screamed, "That's no bald eagle—it's a crow with an A&W chip bag on its head!"

And so it was. The crow flapped leisurely away and the now empty container of French fries fluttered lightly down onto the hood of our truck.

We had so badly wanted it to be a bald eagle. Sadly, our focus now shifted towards the greasy remnant lying before us.
Everyone sighed loudly.

Perfect example of appearance vs reality right?

Perhaps not nearly as deep and philosophical as you might have expected from my grand opening, but then I've never held false illusions of myself as anyone too grand or philosophical.

So, as we sally forth into another week I admonish you to always keep this simple truth in mind and don't jump to hasty conclusions; things are not always what they appear.

Hair Dos... and Don'ts

Sometimes the latest hair trends leave me baffled.

Take a recent one for boys. Both sides are razored off close to the head, leaving hair, in roughly a three-inch wide strip, long.

So long, in fact, it can be braided or put into a short and highly unusual ponytail. If, however, it's left to its own devices, the hair lops over one eye interfering with the child's vision.

This requires a frequent, exaggerated flicking motion to allow a brief window of sight.

Naturally, any discomfort, displacement of the spinal column or associated whiplash is all worthwhile in order to achieve the proper effect.

When I was a kid there was no allowance made for personal expression. There were no outlandish hairstyles or wild colors for this girl.

No keeping the current fashion or following the looks promoted by movie stars.

For me, haircuts consisted of a hurried trip to an elderly hairdresser who obtained her license back in the '30s—to a darkened shop where all who entered, later exited with identical coiffures.

Everyone looked like Marg Osburne. Good ol' Marg who, while quite the songstress on Don Messer's Jubilee had an old lady hairdo: short, rolled, fluffed and then one lone curl was sprayed into place high over her left eye.

This was fine for Marg, but I was 12!

I remember one fateful visit that saw me hunched fearfully in the truck for as long as possible, arguing that I liked hair in my eyes. I was finally hauled through the door, plunked in her chair, a cape was flung over my shaking shoulders and the hairdresser advanced upon me brandishing her gleaming implements. One hour later, after what remained of my hair was set, teased, backcombed and I had coughed through a lavish application of spray, I recall dashing out to the truck to consult my reflection in the rear-view mirror.

Moaning in horror I took it all in. Yup, no doubt about it, there she was—Marg Osburne in all her glory.

My young daughter has her own ideas on hairstyles and, avoiding a repeat of the "Marg" era, I gave in when she stated her desire for blue hair. It actually looked quite pretty. She was happy, I was happy, the stylist was happy. There were congratulations all round until next morning when she woke up looking like a blueberry!

The color had seeped into every fiber of her being. Her face was blue, neck, ears and hands were blue. Pillow, bed, and clothing—all blue. I trust you've heard of the, "Midas touch"? Well, try it in a lovely shade of aquamarine. To make matters worse, she was scheduled to perform in a high school theater event that night!

I sat with trepidation in the audience as she entered the stage under bright spotlights. Turning, she faced the crowd and an audible gasp went up from the assembly. My girl looked positively radioactive. Throughout the performance she raised indigo arms to gesture, peacock hands fluttered gracefully to illustrate her words and teeth flashed in brilliant white relief against her Smurf-like face. I guess that's one way to make a fashion statement.

Yes, interesting hairstyles will always be around, but thankfully hair grows back, color fades and I will never again resemble Marg Osburne.

God willing.

I Go Out Walkin' After Midnight...

 Patsy Cline had the right idea when she crooned the words above.

 If you choose an evening in summer when the sky is crystal clear, the moon rides high, and the fractious breeze has soothed itself to sleep, the world becomes a magical place to ramble.

 And I'm not suggesting you trudge down streets in town with overhead lights flooding the scene, or along gravel roads where vehicles never cease their heedless rush. No, I'm proposing you follow a well-worn cow path that winds through a meadow behind the barn, or perhaps meander down a grassy trail past a sighing field of wheat.

 Places such as these capture my fancy; places that are reflective and quiet.

 My daughter and I did just that the other night. It was a little after midnight and the farm lay silent as we stole across the lawn and paused on our bridge among the cattails. They've flourished this year with all the rain, leaving only a small space open where the creek gurgles.

 A full moon glimmered in the dark ripples and lent a soft glow to willows that line the shore; their craggy tops set in sharp relief against the silver sphere above.

We hopped off the opposite side and wound our way through clover, its scent heavy and cloying, eventually finding ourselves in the cow pasture.

Of course, there's a certain risk involved when following a groove worn into the earth by cattle, particularly when sight is limited and one is wearing pink running shoes, but these are trivial matters of no consequence on such a night.

Coyotes wailed in the east. It was an eerie sound in the still of the night, but much friendlier than the dreadful hum of mosquitoes in our ears.

After strolling past the oat crop, we ended by flopping down on a hill overlooking the yard.

You can see clear up to the Fartown Hills from there, and the lights of our neighbors winked at us.

We lolled on grass damp with dew, and talked, and gazed at the stars until we began to feel as though we weren't alone. Tiny flickering lights appeared in the warm air around us, and I told Aliyah a story of fireflies and her brother, Chris.

It was a summer, years ago, on a family visit to Sifton, Manitoba. There always seemed to be plenty of lightening bugs in the countryside where my uncles lived (also ticks, but that's another story with none of the pleasant overtones I'm trying to convey).

Ten-year-old Chris happily bounded though the yard on the evening in question, collecting the inoffensive bugs in a jar. These flashy little insects use their light to attract a mate, so around bedtime I called a halt to Chris' interference in their search for love. I told him to set them free and come inside.

"But it took me SO long to catch them all," he protested loudly, "I don't wanna let them go."

He clutched the Mason jar to his chest dramatically, and slowly edged out of arms reach.

Typically, the mom in me responded, "Those bugs will die if you keep them cooped up all night. Let them loose." I turned dismissively and focused my efforts on washing the rosy faces of his younger siblings before hustling them off to bed.

A short time later, Chris dragged his sorry self through the living room and turned listless, empty eyes towards me.

"They're gone," he mumbled, his voice trembling with emotion. I felt a pang of guilt as I beheld the stooped figure of my son, bent with untold grief, ascending the staircase to his room.

Maybe I should have let him keep one, I thought, closing the door to my own bedroom later that night. Poor kid, he doesn't ask for much.

Mentally berating myself for crushing an innocent lad's simple request for a couple of bugs, I flipped off the light and lay down.

Wait—was that a light I saw in the corner? Nah, couldn't be. Hang on—there it was again. It flickered right, and then flashed left, and then two more joined in.

Suddenly my room was filled with the blinking lights of fireflies! Innocent lad be damned, that little varmint purposely released them in my bedroom!

I hollered his name and the door opened a smidgen. A pair of small lips were pressed to the crack, "Well—you didn't say where to let them go."

Aliyah and I giggled on the hilltop as I painted her this picture; our folded arms for pillows and the fireflies and stars our only companions.

Times like these are hard to beat.

I go out walkin'...

Rednecks

It was as I sat with my Uncle Don and Aunt Esther on their deck in Sifton, Manitoba that I recalled a famous quote by Jeff Foxworthy.

Why would spending quality time with my beloved family cause such thoughts to come to mind, you ask? The answer was as simple as looking up.

Flapping smartly in the wayward summer breeze above us, a lovely 16-in. x 20-in. blue tarpaulin was slung from the house to a few nearby bushes.

This "sunshade", while lacking a certain aesthetic component, did the job, and though it crinkled loudly, inferring with our conversation, it did nothing to dampen our spirits as we quaffed cool drinks from the Mason jars we held.

Don, lounging in a wicker rocking chair, fanned himself with a ratty old fly swatter, its fraying edges bound up with duct tape.

Here's the deal—my Uncle's a redneck.

Reclining with him in the shade, I glanced toward the many pots of flowers that lined the stairs and path to their garage. Esther's favorite color is red and the plants were flourishing, but—what were the tall green spikes that grew among the crimson petals?

"Oh, those are onions," my uncle answered with quiet pride.

"Want one?" Deftly he leaned forward and plucked a particularly lush specimen, peeled it back and sunk his teeth into the crunchy white flesh.

"No, I don't WANT one," I replied in disgust. I mean, fine, the man enjoys eating raw onions, but isn't planting them among the petunias taking things a bit far?

Certainty not, I was told, and watched with a revolted sort of fascination as he crunched his way through to the green tips and settled back in his chair.

"See that tree in the neighbor's yard?" he pointed behind me with one long green frond. "Couple years ago it needed trimming. Right at the top. Wanna know how I did it?" Hesitantly, I nodded. "Shotgun," he said shortly, and began to slowly rock.

Apparently other branches had been successfully trimmed by his brother Richard (also a redneck) who shimmied up the truck carrying a sharp saw, but the very top was too dangerous to handle that way.

A small crowd gathered to assess the problem (since the yard was situated in the middle of their small town) but no solutions were found until my uncle brought out the ole twelve gauge and blasted the trunk clear through.

It toppled heavily to earth amid a round of applause, warm handshakes and a telephone call from the local Credit Union who thought they were about to be robbed.

Laughing, I mentioned that there was no doubt about it—he was a classic redneck.

"So—what? You think you're exempt?" he questioned with raised eyebrows.

The laughter froze on my lips and—despite the warmth of the day—a cold chill trickled down my spine,

Casting my thoughts inward, I remembered only last week when, in preparation for the arrival of some special visitors from England, I'd hauled out the old Electrolux, stood on a chair, and vacuumed the ceiling.

Then later that same day, whilst outside burning a bit of trash, daughter Aliyah appeared at my elbow bearing marshmallows and roasting sticks. "No sense wasting a good fire," she'd said, threading a puffy treat onto the wire.

Crud. He's right. We've got it too.

Signs of the Times

Signs are everywhere. Quietly they hang around, advising the public of information it may or may not be interested in. Recently, however, I saw two great ones that gave me a chuckle.

The first was while visiting Germany this summer. As we made our way about that wonderful country, I noticed large placards on every street and motorway boldly proclaiming the word *Ausfahrt*; meaning exit.

What a great word! Immediately I hastened to use it myself; seeing the multitude of applications for it in our own language (changing the meaning of course).

Consider substituting it in for other, infinitely more common and ignoble words people use every day. You'll understand what I mean in a moment.

Upon observing a pack of unruly children pillaging your raspberry bushes in the backyard, you could easily lean out the screen door and yell: "Hey! You little ausfahrts get outta my garden."

Doesn't that seem kinder somehow? And no less effective?

Or how about a wife slowly turning before her husband with a soft pleading in her eyes to ask, "Honey, do these jeans make my ausfahrt look big?" Sounds a little more refined, don't you think? Less crass.

Let's take a final example: When the government pushes through legislation you don't agree with, perhaps—oh I don't know—let's say the legalization of an illicit drug—you can gather together with like-minded neighbors over coffee and say with concern, "Those ausfahrts in parliament have no bloody idea."

See how well it works?

The next sign was taped to the wall at eye level as I took my seat in the dentist's chair.

Please refrain from cell phone use during dental procedures.

I lifted questioning eyebrows to the fellow as he advanced upon me with a gleaming syringe.

Shrugging expressively, he explained through his mask, "People take selfies."

This raises several disturbing questions, not to mention images.

Let's try to picture how it might play out.

A young woman slides into the dentist's chair with trepidation, firmly clutching her best friend—the phone. She is instructed to lie back and open wide as the gowned and masked figures of the dentist and an assistant bend over her head, adjusting a 10,000-watt spotlight on her gaping mouth.

The dentist raises his tiny, yet powerful drill and lowers it into the rotting cavity with the sound of a thousand droning bees, as the assistant busily sucks flying chunks of decayed matter and saliva from around the woman's tongue and cheeks.

At that precise moment, she wedges her arm up between the two professionals to a point above her face, and shoots a rapid succession of photos.

Later, family and friends on Facebook, view the photos above the caption, "Only two cavities."

First of all, who the heck cares about your cavities? Secondly, who in their right mind wants to memorialize this event? Why in the name of all that is holy, would you take a picture of yourself, flat on your back with your mouth stretched to full, unpleasant capacity, while a power drill grinds into your blackened, decomposing teeth and your bubbling spittle is vacuumed down a plastic tube?

It's beyond me, but I guess if this situation refers to you, you may well think I'm a complete ausfahrt for making fun of this important event.

Sorry. I call 'em how I see 'em.

The Gift of Family

Family reunions spring up everywhere over the summer months, particularly on the farm. Gatherings in the countryside allow folks enough room to park a holiday camper, start an impromptu game of softball or at least let kids and dogs run and play without the boundaries of streets and traffic.

For some people it's the only chance they'll ever get to experience a taste of life on the farm and their visit can, at times, turn into a guided tour.

For others it's simply an opportunity to kick back and relax with loved ones who are otherwise only seen at weddings and funerals.

Yes, it's true, we're hosting a family reunion this summer, and preparations have begun early to ensure everyone has a fabulous time.

One of the main components, in my mind at least, is the food.

Many moons ago I began laboring over elaborate feasts for friends and family. I'd fall asleep at night with a cookbook clutched in my weary hand, while hastily scribbled notes and meal plans lay scattered about the house on whatever bits of paper I could find at the moment.

The backs of envelopes were pressed into service, Aliyah's schoolwork was often returned to the teacher with recipes for things like Creamy Garden Slaw scrawled on the back, and ingredient lists were plastered across bills and tax returns making them pretty much illegible.

My husband Tom would sit at the table, waving rumpled papers in my face with exasperation, "Helen! What the heck do we owe the phone company? Two cups of finely grated carrots?"

But I digress. These elaborate culinary creations resulted in a precedent being set, and now people arrive at my home with expectations. Rats.

Not every dish has turned out as well as expected. There were the Parmesan Salad Cups that presented themselves in a glossy magazine photo as being "easy as pie" to prepare.

For a start, I've never found that making a good pie was all that simple, but in the picture a beaming, and beautifully appointed woman bore them to a table of enthusiastic guests who applauded their arrival.

They sat on tiny white porcelain plates (the cheese cups not the guests) looking like lacy vessels of toasted, cheesy goodness as they brimmed with an assortment of spring greens.

My efforts were not nearly so lovely; the cheese stuck stubbornly to my baking sheet, refusing to come quietly.

Once pried up, none folded effortlessly around the

glass that was used to form the bowl-like shape. They chose instead to stiffen and stick out at right angles like disobedient children told to finish their peas.

Needless to say, there was no cheering as I hurriedly dumped each one in front of a startled guest. While tasty, they resembled a brown mat that had been left in the rain too long and curled around the edges under the summer sun.

Back to reunions, I know Dad enjoys these events to no end. He spoke of it only last night, clapping me on the back with a resounding thump and grinning broadly.

"It's gonna be great to see everyone again hey Helen?"

I peered at him through bleary eyes, images of cakes and pies super-imposing themselves over his face.

"Yeah, great," I repeated with a trace of bitterness.

It's all very easy for the patriarch I must say. The man who only has to throw on a smile, a clean shirt, and scuffle 43 feet across the yard in his bloody bedroom slippers to attend the whole shindig!

Nonetheless, it will be fun, and most of me is looking forward to it. We have fine musicians in the family, which will brighten up evenings spent around a blazing fire.

My son, Justin Walker, plays fiddle, guitar and harmonica with skill, and sings an eclectic repertoire of songs.

Uncle Don Gessner has an old-time country band in Manitoba and his music has entertained groups for many years. Family will join together with love and laughter, hugs and a few tears, while special memories are forged and acquaintance is not forgot.

As we draw closer to the warmth of the flame and reminisce about loved ones who join us in spirit only, we are thankful for this time together.

Family is truly a gift.

Teenagers!

The other night, at approximately 1:20 a.m., I awoke from pleasant slumber to wander groggily from my bed for a glass of water. Feeling for the bedroom door, I padded silently from the room. Suddenly, a small shriek and the clatter of falling metal pans split the air. I froze in my tracks. Who was there?

While this could describe the opening scene from some late night crime drama, in fact was only my teenage daughter foraging for food in a dimly lit kitchen.

"What in the world are you doing?" I exclaimed in wide-eyed astonishment, coming fully awake to take in the scene. She stood at the stove, heating an electric griddle and preparing the dry ingredients for a batch of pancakes.

"Your father and I didn't see hide nor hair of you all day! Were you lying in wait till we went to bed so you could creep out under cover of darkness and fry flapjacks?"

Alas, this sort of bizarre behavior is not new. It happens all the time. I put it down to her being a teen.

Our daughter's so attached to her bed, it almost seems a waste to take her on a holiday. On the last European adventure, we struggled each morning to wake her up and get her out the door.

If we'd supplied her with blankets, Ramen noodles and an electric cord to charge her device, we could have stayed in a cardboard box on the edge of town and she'd never have known the difference.

Of course, we aren't alone. I hear other parents complain their teenager's text, tweet, snap or whatever the heck it is they do until sunrise, and then sprawl like lumps in bed till past midday.

I also know parental requests are met with exaggerated groans, rolling of eyes or an interesting combination of the two, and homework reminders are treated with the same outright horror as if they'd been asked to step in the back yard and butcher a cow.

Still, I dread the day she leaves for university, although, I suppose, not much will change.

We seldom look upon her face.

One evening, my husband, Tom, grumbled he'd gone to call her for the evening meal, but was unable to locate the girl beneath the mountains of discarded clothing that litter her room, so he'd given up.

I hastened to assure him she had to be in there somewhere. After all, I'd just removed a heavy tray of dishes from the table beside her bed and some of the congealed food left behind had looked quite recent.

"She's there alright," I comforted the man, patting his hand. "She'll soon get hungry and crawl from her hole. If only we could stay up late enough to catch her," I finished wistfully.

Several weeks later, we flinched in surprise as a tall, dark-haired girl appeared in the living room where we slouched on the sofa watching TV.

"Who are you?" Tom squinted doubtfully at the teen. "Aliyah?"

"It's her alright," I whispered at his elbow. "She has your eyes."

Oh well, it's not quite that bad.

I'd gladly pick up dishes and dirty laundry for another 17 years if I could keep her at home.

Our teenager has been an absolute joy and we love her to bits. If only—just once—she'd clean her room.

You're Only as Old as You Feel

Am I getting old?

Hang on! Before you respond and are never forgiven, keep in mind it was purely a rhetorical question. I don't really want an answer. It's just—this week in particular I was made keenly aware of my years. However, as they say, age is only a number.

For example, Julia (Hurricane) Hawkins is a 103 year old lady who competed in the USA National Senior Games 100-metre dash in 2019. What a woman. Apparently, Hawkins has always been a cyclist and likes to live simply but healthfully.

The most amazing information was, apart from, as she said, "…running from the garden to get the phone when it rings…" she only began this journey in track and field three years ago, when she turned 100.

This woman is an inspiration. She certainly didn't let age dictate her ability.

However, for me this week began its downward spiral with a commercial on TV. I was happily preparing a salad for supper, but glanced up when the announcer said, "Seniors 50 and over can take advantage of new transit…" Listening in growing horror, the lettuce I was holding dropped to the floor at my feet as I listened to the unfolding scene.

Images on the screen, depicted frail, white haired ladies shuffling out to the door of a gleaming new bus where some guy with a smart suit and insincere smile took their arthritic hands and guided their stumbling feet aboard his craft.

All movements were slow, calculated and deliberate. The participants of the commercial sported sensible orthopedic footwear, elasticized slacks and pastel cardigans edged in lace.

"Are you kidding me?" I said aloud in amazement, "Fifty?" My indignation grew by the second as I retrieved the offended greens and thrust them angrily under the tap, "I might be persuaded to drive the bloody bus, but you'd never catch me riding in it," I growled savagely.

My decline down the slippery slope to premature aging escalated when, after injuring my back picking raspberries last week (sounds crazy, I know) the simplest of activities became insurmountable; stuff like walking and standing up.

Then, the very next day, I had to go pick up my girl from a lake where she was visiting family. Leveraging myself behind the wheel, with effort, I drove to a nearby town to fuel up. It took me five minutes and a lot of whimpering to get one leg out the door—while employees at the gas station watched in fascination—then another five to put it back once I realized it couldn't be done. They raised questioning hands to accompany puzzled looks as I nodded self-consciously to them on exiting.

Once home again I sat a prisoner of my vehicle, staring at

the flight of stairs up to my deck. Could they be conquered?

The viability of quickly installing an Acorn Stair Lift crossed my mind, and I could see myself gliding effortlessly up the steps with a saintly smile plastered on my face just like those happy folks on TV.

But, first things first: how the heck to get out of the car?

By increments I inched myself around and was tentatively extending a leg when every muscle seized, I slid from my seat with a screech, and tumbled heavily to the ground.

I lay prone upon God's good earth, pondering my fate. Where's the *Littlest Hobo*[*] when you needed him? The Hobo would trot purposefully to my side with a small step stool or perhaps a strong wooden cane gripped in his teeth. Then lie patiently by my side offering moral support and quiet strength until I was able to rise.

Or maybe Lassie[**] would appear! Lassie would take one look at my miserable prostrate figure and run for help, her long, freshly brushed fur flowing in the breeze. She'd grasp some unsuspecting person by the hand, and with several low "woofs" lead them to my grateful side.

Our own dog, Chili, sniffed hopefully at my pockets for anything edible, then finding nothing, stepped over my motionless body and trotted briskly off down the driveway to visit the neighbors. Bloody dog.

Thankfully, in time I was able to crawl pitifully into my

house and expire on the living room floor.

My 87-year-old father assured me, through a phone call from the tractor, he'd come haul me to my feet if need be, but would rather get in a full day's work.

Sigh. He's another spry, fit person. So, there I lay sightlessly staring at the ceiling using the time to consider my immediate and somewhat bleak future.

To add further insult, later that night, as I hunched painfully off to bed, my beloved granddaughter, Anna, suggested the immediate purchase of a walker.

Summoning every bit of strength at my limited disposal, I raised an arm to throw something at her, but clearly it's too late for me.

Save yourselves people, I'll just lie here quietly waiting for the first snow to cover me up.

You're only as old as you feel—and man, do I feel old.

* The Littlest Hobo was a popular television show in the 70s and early 80s. The main character was a German Shepard that traveled throughout Canada performing good deeds.

** Come on—everyone knows Lassie.

Welcome Back

Well, hang on to your hat, because another school year is about to begin.

It seems only a short time ago kids anxiously waited for the last day of class in June so they could run screaming with glee from the hallowed halls of learning, and fling themselves on the sofa at home to moan, "I'm bored."

However, before memories wash away like sand from under the swing set, I'd like to take a moment to share a few bright spots from the past year.

One of my favorite jobs is to help kids learn spelling, punctuation and sentence structure.

Needless to say, it's not their favorite job.

Before the term ended, I went with a small group to a nearby town for an Industrial Arts class. There was already a large group of kids busily tapping on computers as we entered the room, and I wandered about the area looking over their shoulders.

Pausing beside one boy, I leaned in and spoke to him, "None of your sentences begin with capital letters. Please change them." He twisted round slowly and deliberately to peer up into my face with surprise.

"What?" he asked in a disbelieving tone, a frown forming over his eyes. "This is shop class. It doesn't matter."

"It always matters," I replied crisply. "Please correct it." Moving away, I overheard him whispering to one of my boys seated nearby, who then turned to him and sighed deeply. "Look, we call her the grammar police at my school so you might as well do what she says. It's easier that way—trust me."

As I assist them in editing their writing, I often find sentences interesting in more ways than one.

I've jotted down three:
1. My grate grandmother died of oldness.
2. Are nayber had a hard attack.
3. His granny lives in a nursery home.

Of course, we all hope to, one day die simply of "oldness" and who can dispute the fact heart attacks are a hard bloody business?

Furthermore, perhaps, if when reaching a certain age, we were allowed entrance into nursery homes, complete with colorful plastic toys, a sandbox and wax crayons, our declining years might be a whole lot more fun.

As my bus pulled away from school one day, I noticed a young lad pause at the closest intersection and assume a rather distinctive pose.

Without a moment's hesitation he dropped his drawers and aimed a thin, yellow stream at a stop sign that stood, minding its own business, on the corner.

Was this rash behavior a premeditated indictment upon traffic laws and restrictive signposts everywhere? Was it some anti-establishment act of rebellion against school and its overbearing authority in his young life?

Or was it merely a small boy of six caring not for the conventions of society and the niceties of indoor plumbing? A boy disinterested in finding the concealment necessary to disguise such a deed; a boy unconcerned with the condemnation of an unwilling public forced to witness this performance (namely, a bus-load of kids yelling, "EEEW!")

Alas, we shall never know.

Tammy?

The school I work at recently held "Spirit Days".

The kids dressed up as historical figures, hillbillies, and their favorite singers. In preparing for this last event, I pawed through my closet until a familiar glimmer drew me to the item I sought: the notorious Tammy Wynette jacket.

I fingered the material lovingly.

Tammy can't be held responsible for the garishness of the thing. She was merely the inspiration when I named it.

It was purchased back in the 80s when shoulder pads were "in" and sequins the rage. When every square inch of cloth was bedazzled with cheap rhinestones, glittery baubles and silver trim. It was ostentatious, grandiose and loud. I loved it.

Sadly, there isn't much call to wear it anymore, unless as a costume. Its day is done, but I can't throw it away. It holds memories.

The last time I had it on was back in 1997 when I was asked to stand up as bridesmaid for the wedding of a woman I didn't know too well. Not sure why she even asked me, but I agreed to be part of her special day, and packing up my son, who was only eight, I motored off to the big city to meet with her and her betrothed, Fredrick.

At the last moment, I'd pulled on my Tammy Wynette jacket, foolishly thinking I'd blend in with other well-dressed women in the thriving metropolis, and wouldn't stand out like I was angling to win a Liberace look-alike contest. Wrong. That's exactly what I looked like—or worse.

Stepping out of my car in the parking lot where we'd agreed to meet, I acknowledged the friend and her fiancé. I hadn't seen her in years and she'd changed—a lot.

Her hair was bleached platinum blonde and puffed out around her head much like the top of a Q-tip. She'd applied so much self-tanner she looked positively orange, and she wore a short, white, unbelievably tight dress with matching five-inch heeled stilettos.

Wow.

Then, Fredrick unfolded himself from an expensive black car. He was a great Adonis of a man, probably 6'-4", with golden hair that curled across broad shoulders and tumbled halfway down his back. Gleaming white teeth shone from a similarly tanned face as he stepped forward to wring my hand. He wore a long, fringe leather jacket, embroidered with dragons and multi-colored flowers, tight jeans and brown, suede, knee-high boots.

Is this taking on a touch of unreality for you yet? Try being me.

We made quite a spectacle a few moments later as we strode purposefully into a fabric shop to buy material for bridesmaid dresses.

Customers stopped mid-sentence and swung about to watch our grand entrance, jaws dropped, and small children stood silently beside their mothers to gaze at us with wide, fascinated eyes. A clerk shrank behind the till as Fredrick's booming voice requested a bolt of peach-colored satin.

Afterward, when we exited the store in a flourish of sequins, stilettos, leather and hair, I knew what they were thinking as their eyes rested on the small, ordinary boy in our midst. "Poor little blighter. Wonder which of those hookers is his mom?"

Despite this embarrassing memory, the Tammy Wynette jacket shall not be tossed.

As she so famously sang, "We're Gonna Hold On". She wasn't really referring to a woman and her flamboyant coat, but I'm taking it that way.

Nuggets of Gold

A few short days ago found me tapping away on my computer in a happy haze of sunshine yellow. My writing room had been gilded in that glow since frost magically transformed the bluff of poplar trees, near my window, into the rich shades of autumn. As I work, I love to gaze outside, at any time of year, but fall is especially lovely. Then came high winds, pelting rain and now the recent snow which stripped my leafy friends bare, leaving only stark reminders of the glory that was. However, in every season, as in every situation, there are always things to be thankful for or to smile about. We just have to keep our eyes peeled for these golden moments.

One aspect of life that's always gratifying for me is my job driving a school bus. Perched in my lofty seat it's always a joy to view the passage of each season; from smooth, rolling mounds of snow glittering with a morning frost, to fields of verdant grain, churning like the Atlantic in a wild gale.

Also a privilege is the time I spend with children. They are precious little people indeed.

Two weeks past, I pulled the bus up to a house, stopped, and flung open the doors for a sweet little blond-haired girl to clamber aboard. I know for absolute certain she's a sweet little girl because she told me so quite distinctly.

On this particular day she bounded eagerly up the steps clasping tiny hands together to protect some secret, prized possession. Eyes shining with excitement, she paused beside me and breathlessly asked if I'd like to see. I imagined it was perhaps a sparkly rock, a toy or even a candy—anything but what it really was.

With great ceremony she slowly uncovered her prize. As she did so, a vile brown liquid began to seep through her fingers and drip to the bus floor.

Good grief, what was it?

With a final flourish she revealed her treasure! An enormous, dead June bug lay on its back across her outstretched palms; spindly legs folded in death across its middle and bodily fluids trickling from a blackened abdomen.

"ACKK," I screeched, lurching away in revulsion. However, noting her immediate distress, I recovered myself quickly. "I mean—WOW!—what a fine looking beetle you have there! And so juicy," I added, as we both peered down at the unpleasant puddle forming below.

"Now, how about we clean you up a bit." YIKES! Bring on the disinfectant.

Likewise, another noteworthy situation took place driving home after school. Glancing up to my bus mirror to check on the children, I noticed a pair of sparkling, thoughtful brown eyes hovering just above a seat several rows back.

At length, the little girl spoke. "Mrs. Toews, did you know I lost my toque today?" she queried importantly, in the manner of one interrogating a delinquent member of the Legislative Assembly.

Naturally, I'm well accustomed to receiving this sort of monumental news flash, and I responded appropriately—with shock and alarm.

"Good heavens, you don't say! It wasn't in your coat pocket or your locker?" I hollered back to her over the din of the rumbling vehicle.

"No," Lelu replied, a puzzled look on her face, clearly questioning her decision to share this critical information with one so daft.

She continued, "It fell on the floor beside my chair. Everyone helped me look, but no one could find it."

Now it was my turn to look confused as I imagined this group of incompetent youngsters milling blindly around her desk, hopelessly incapable of spotting a bright green hat.

"What about your teacher?" I yelled optimistically, "Maybe she saw it."

Lelu hollered in response: "Teacher gave me a tissue to wrap it in because of the blood, but it fell out somewhere."

She turned away, losing interest in the discussion since only one of the two participants understood what the heck was going on.

"The blood? A tissue?" I repeated to myself in wonder.

It certainly seemed like a cavalier attitude had been taken to what clearly must have been some form of head injury for this child. The girl sustained trauma to her noggin, lost enough blood to stain her toque, but all she was allotted were a few disposable tissues—for the hat?

Suddenly her tiny face popped up above the seat once more and she grinned broadly.

"See," she shouted, pointing to a large gap in her smile where a tooth had recently exited.

"A TOOTH!" I yelled in relief. "You lost a TOOTH today. Congratulations," and both beaming happily we continued on down the road.

There you go. Proof positive if we watch carefully, there are fascinating and often humorous situations taking place all around us.

Whatever your circumstance today, I know a nugget of gold will glimmer in the midst of darkness if you can see it. There's always something to be grateful for.

Even a dead bug can be a good thing—emphasis on DEAD.

You Are Entering the Hunt Zone

Autumn is the fulfillment of a years' work for a farmer, and everything rides on it.

Will the weather cooperate long enough to finish combining or will early snow buffet the land before crops are safely under cover? It's an age-old question with no way of knowing the answer. Of course, along with the thrum of combines working in the field and a crisp edge in the air, this time of year also brings back scads of waterfowl heading south, and the inevitable hunting season begins.

You might as well know, I'm not exactly a fan of the sport. My sons have learned to tread lightly around me when it comes to their own bloodthirsty ways—making it hard to comprehend why they would ever dream of asking ME to accompany them duck hunting. I think Chris asked me on a whim; never expecting I'd agree, but I thought of it solely as precious time spent with my boys. (Also, I have to admit, I was hoping to warn the ducks.)

As a sliver of light edged over the horizon, I stepped outside behind Justin. Immediately, a frigid October wind sliced through my thin coat.

"Hold it!" I announced. Marching back inside, I applied four more sweaters, three pairs of long underwear, ski pants, two hats and my husband's enormous canvas coat, oh, and some furry gauntlets like people wear snowmobiling when it's -40C. Now, I was ready.

Chris could be seen tapping his steering wheel impatiently by the time I plodded heavily to the truck.

I swung each leg out stiffly in a sweeping motion: arms slashing, each step calculated, robotic and deliberate.

"Help," I said feebly as I paused rigidly beside the back door of his enormous 4x4. My loving sons lifted me up, tossed me into the back seat and we rumbled off across the brown prairie grass.

Pulling up to the edge of a slough west of our farm, Chris parked near a forest of tall rustling cattails. The men hopped out, shouldered their shotguns and strode over to a canoe secreted beneath a tarp in the weeds.

"What's this?" I demanded sharply, "No one said anything about a boat." My boys know I have a dreadful fear of water.

"What if we tip?" I whine. "I'm sporting fifty pounds of extra clothing. I'll go down like a rock!"

"We'll drag you out—eventually," Justin assured me nastily, holding out a hand from the boat to help me board.

Sadly, there comes a time in every parent's life where the tables turn and the parent becomes the child. This was mine.

Grimly I held each side of the flimsy craft and moaned

softy with each surge forward into the murky water.

"Stop whimpering," Justin hissed, "You'll scare away the birds."

They rowed into an area thick with rushes before we stopped to take up arms. Well, they took up arms, I hunkered miserably between them thinking of my soft bed at home.

Suddenly, quacking could be heard and the whooshing sound of many wings heading our way.

BANG! BANG! Shots rang out beside me and a bird plummeted from the sky. Then another dropped in a tangle of wings and splashed into the water.

"Oh no," I cried in distress, "Those poor, defenseless ducks. There they were innocently flapping along, and you cut them from the sky. I'll bet they had loving families too—wives, husbands, maybe children that will have to forge onward in their lonely journey south without mom and dad. All so you can gnaw on their sad little bones at the dinner table." I looked accusingly at my sons as they picked up oars to begin retrieval of the birds.

"Jeez, now I feel guilt," said Justin, gazing toward the protruding feathers. His rowing ceased.

"Alright, that's it," Chris rounded on me with a scowl. "You've been nothing but trouble all morning. Either you sit quietly, or we row you back to shore and you can wait in the truck." He turned decisively to lift a bedraggled bird from the waves; watching with immense satisfaction as its life force ebbed away and it went on to that great duck pond in the sky. (Exaggeration for effect.)

I shrank down and was silent.

"I suppose this isn't a good time to tell you I have to pee?" I ventured moments later, peering up from beneath my two hats.

Yes, hunting season may come again, but it'll take place without me.

I'll enjoy watching flocks of mallards winging by overhead, the occasional group of Sandhill cranes flapping slowly past, or hear geese honking late at night over on the slough, but I won't go hunting again.

Doubt if I'd be asked.

Women Drivers

I've heard the unpleasant generalizations out there touting all women as bad drivers, and I think its rubbish.

I suppose some credibility in that statement will be lost due to the fact I may be a tad biased, but honestly, statistics prove me right.

Admittedly, there are several differences in driving styles between the two sexes, one marked difference being that in stressful situations men tend to be more aggressive whereas women might become overly careful and wary. At times, especially in youthful zeal, this tendency may lead men to take dangerous risks and alternately women might appear slow and unsure, but statistically, women are involved in fewer accidents and receive less traffic violations than men.

However, I'm sure we've all seen varying standards of driving displayed from both sides.

Any discussion of women drivers always makes me think of my years working for Dave cleaning corrals.

Dave was the sort of man who didn't suffer fools gladly. He ran a tight ship—apart from the fact his vessels were a bunch of enormous trucks laden with manure and the waterways navigated were deep cesspools of liquid crap.

He was a hard taskmaster who kept a watchful eye on

every move we made. Employees often didn't last too long working for Dave. Either they didn't like having to adhere to the standards he insisted upon and left, or he fired them for foolish mistakes which could jeopardize people or equipment.

As a woman entering this man's world, I was glad to have a boss who plainly spelled out what was expected (occasionally at the top of his lungs six inches from my nose) where I'd failed and how to correct it. He always treated me fairly. I was given the same opportunity to prove myself as any of the men who came before or after, and I appreciated it.

One crisp autumn day we pulled the trucks into a very neat, organized farmyard. Everyone climbed out to stretch their legs while Dave and the farmer met to discuss what needed to be done.

From the corner of my eye I noticed the man's eyes flick coldly towards me and then dart away. Men were always a little surprised to see a woman hop out of the truck, particularly one who stood on the running board to freshen her lipstick in a side mirror, but they were usually good-natured about it. Somehow though, this case seemed different, and despite the farmer's lowered tones I could hear the conversation clearly.

"I don't want any woman drivin' a truck in my corrals," he stated irritably, flinging an arm wide to indicate his well-ordered yard. "These gates are new and I'm not payin' to have 'em replaced when she backs into 'em, so she can just keep the hell out."

"Not a problem," Dave announced loudly, without batting an eye. He whirled around and marched swiftly back to where we stood in shocked silence, "Get back in your trucks. We're leaving," he said curtly. The farmer, clearly stunned by this unforeseen turn of events, hurriedly jogged toward him in protest.

"Hey wait a minute," he now wheedled, plastering a sickly smile on his face, "I didn't say you ALL had to leave—just HER. I want my corrals cleaned."

Dave leaned an elbow out the window as he gunned the motor of his truck, and threw the vehicle into reverse. He fixed the farmer with a piercing stare and addressed him in no uncertain terms, "That woman over there is part of my crew. She's one of the best drivers I've had and if she goes, we all go. End of story."

That was Dave. I felt such gratitude mingled with pride that he had stuck up for me in this way that a tear almost escaped, but I nabbed it just in time since we truck drivers never like to display overt sentimentality.

In the end, the man capitulated, did a little groveling, and we stayed. Although I'm sure he didn't like it, I worked there all that day—fences and gates safe and accounted for when we left.

Overall, I don't believe any one group of drivers is superior to another. It all boils down to the individual. As is with most skills acquired in life, there are always people who will excel and people who just muddle through.

Now, if you'd like to trade stories on larger-than-life employers, I've got some dandies …

Second-hand Style

Cooler weather always brings out shivers and sweaters, and while participating in this recent transition from one season to another, I found myself considering how effortlessly we discard clothing, and rush to purchase more.

According to what I've read, each person tosses out about 36 kilos (80 lbs.) of clothing per year. That figure also includes things like towels and sheets, but it's still a staggering number. Of course, some garments will be donated to shelters or to second-hand stores for resale, which is a great idea. I remember 20 years ago when I had my first introduction to one of the more well known of these. Memories flood back like yesterday.

In those days I was a single mom and had been asked to a Regimental Ball by a friend who worked for the RCMP. It was a prestigious event and I would be appearing at this well-dressed function wearing—oh no, what would I wear?

I had no money to spend on frivolous frocks. What the heck was I thinking in accepting such an invitation? Closing my eyes with a groan, I visualized stunningly coiffured women sweeping into a ballroom garbed in glittering evening gowns and patent leather stilettos. Jewels sparkled from their throats and beautifully manicured fingers as they turned toward the soft glow of the chandelier to view my lumbering approach.

"Who's the country bumpkin," they'd whisper over colorful cocktails, while reaching to hide empty chairs under the tablecloth as I passed.

I envisioned myself tramping across the dance floor wearing muck-encrusted calving overalls, gumboots and a "Charolais Beef is Best" ball cap. Of course, I wouldn't really attend anything wearing that; my imagination was working overtime. Nonetheless, what was I going to do?

Fortunately, it was several weeks away and on a visit to see family in Manitoba I slumped at the kitchen table sharing my problem with my dear friend Esther.

"I know a thrift store we can go to," she exclaimed in triumph. "You'll find a dress there. Low-priced too."

We rushed into Winnipeg the very next day to pour through racks and racks of dresses. Some were wildly patterned, others grossly outdated, still more were attractive enough, but none had that certain, *je ne sais quoi,* till Esther scraped a few hangers aside and pulled forth a little black number with gold embellishments. She held it up for inspection. It was perfect. It was elegant. It was even designer. But best of all it was cheap!

Later that month I minced up a flight of stairs to the grand event, poise and red lipstick smeared thickly across my face. With carefully constructed aloofness, I smiled kindly upon several women as we all shrugged off jackets and prepared to enter the ballroom.

"What a lovely dress," one gushed appreciatively,

"Wherever did you find it?"

Several others listened in as I replied, waving my arm in a small gesture of indifference, "Oh, this little thing? I picked it up at a Winnipeg boutique recently. It's a Simon Chang."

Turning, I swept from the room, feeling confidence bubble up like champagne—in my five-dollar dress.

Thanks Value Village.

Halloween Hullabaloo

For many generations Canadian children have eagerly anticipated October 31 and all the excitement it entails.

Traditions for this festival have remained much the same over the decades, albeit perhaps they are a little more commercialized these days.

Nonetheless, the fun of Halloween for kids can't be beat, and we grownups enjoy the carefree, playful aspect of it too. I for one, have many fond memories of Halloweens past.

When kids live in the country, such as I did, the job of getting from house to house for treats requires a parent with a vehicle. While such long distances between each farmyard may cut down on the amount of candy kids can cram in a sack, there's still a lot to be said for knowing the folks you visit on Halloween night, and sharing special memories with family, friends and neighbors.

I remember my brother and me making the seven-mile trek to a neighbor's farm each year. Our parents waited in the truck as we rustled noisily up the sidewalk in plastic costumes, our hot breath escaping through ill-fitting masks like Darth Vader during the epic battle against Obi-Wan Kenobi.

Other times we tripped over bed sheets, which trailed along behind us as we struggled to see out of roughly hewn eye-holes. One year my massive sheet was held in place with dad's Western belt. Honestly! Would any self-respecting ghost be caught dead (okay, bad example) cinching itself together with a brown leather strap and the head of a Charolais bull?

But I digress.

The lady of this house always baked the same delicacy; oatmeal cookies sandwiched together with date filling and decorated with orange icing to resemble pumpkins. I hate date filling. Nevertheless, the warm homey atmosphere flooding out to greet us at the door was wonderful and we knew she had made them especially for us, and the other kids who lived nearby. I cherish those memories.

Jumping ahead a few decades, I can tell you I always dress up for my job in some outlandish getup during Halloween. One year I donned a witches' garb (which you may or may not think appropriate depending whether or not you're my ex-husband).

I had worn the flowing black robes and large peaked hat all day and saw no reason to remove them as I drove kids home in the bus after school.

Exiting town, we turned onto one of my better rural roads and eventually lumbered up to speed. After attaining the modest pace of 75-km/h, we began advancing upon an ancient half-ton truck that meandered along the road in front of us. An elderly man slouched behind the wheel, one arm slung out the window as he trundled through the countryside in no particular hurry.

While I am, for the most part, a patient person, I couldn't follow this fellow at the turtle pace of 30-km/h for long.

Taking a moment to secure my trusty headpiece, and ensuring the road ahead was clear, I accelerated and pulled out to pass. As we drew alongside, the man glanced at me through the long windows of the bus door. His face first registered bored indifference and then, after an exaggerated double take, shock and alarm.

I nodded courteously as we motored briskly past in a cloud of dust. Slack jawed, eyes bulging, he gaped out the window in response. His eyes then flitted to the back of the bus looking, no doubt, for innocent children riding helplessly off to their doom. He appeared unaware it was Halloween, and must have had a hair-raising tale to later tell.

"Listen to this Sam; I was in town for cultivator shovels today and you'll never believe what I saw on the way home. A WITCH! I tell you, it was an honest to goodness witch, with the hat and everything. And get this—she was driving a school bus FULL OF KIDS!"

Across our land children have once again enjoyed this thrilling day. Kids know a good thing when they see it.

A million sticky fingers can't be wrong.

Happy Halloween.

Where's My Cane?

As I sit at my desk tonight, the mournful bellowing of recently separated cows and calves echoes through the walls around me, intruding on my thoughtful solitude.

They have a right to complain I guess. It's always a little sad to hear them call for one another, but it's a necessary transition.

Everyone on the farm came together to bring the herd home and begin the process of weaning and weighing the calves. Even my grandson, Kayden, took part. Living in town, he doesn't get a lot of exposure to such happenings, and it was all very interesting.

Unfortunately the weather was cloudy, cold and miserable, which was not ideal since the whole process puts a lot of stress on young stock. To keep everything running as calmly as possible, each person had a specific job, but my brother Bill really shone.

After watching only a little of his impressive skill at working cattle, I believe even Dr. Temple Grandin, the cattle whisperer, would approve. Smoothly anticipating every move the cattle made, he worked with agility, causing me to remark he would have made a darn fine cutting horse.

Kayden watched these activities from a perch high atop a plank fence. Cows jostled one another below, staring wild-eyed at the people surrounding them, and at the unsteady scale they were expected to enter.

There was a liberal supply of both bawling and liquid manure to be found, with the latter splattered generously over every available surface. For a time this became a rather repellent topic of conversation. My boy had plenty of questions and I was on hand to answer them all, since my role that day was little more than of a photo journalist.

However, what kind of crummy photographer shows up without her camera, I asked Kayden as we prepared to enter one of the corrals.

Dashing off, I tore through the gate, peeled cross a pasture and bounded across the sad little bridge spanning Dead Horse Creek. I wanted to make sure I captured all the action on film, so I hustled.

Breathlessly, I returned moments later, to be informed with sadistic enjoyment by my brother that Kayden had watched my speedy departure with growing wonder.

Eyes wide with shock and awe, he clutched the top rail and then, turning to his uncle, expressed measurable surprise that his grandmother was still able to run.

"What's this?" I questioned resentfully, once I'd heard of his astonishment. "I suppose you think I trail around all day in carpet slippers and a bathrobe, unable to drag my brittle bones past a slow shuffle?"

"No, no grandma," he hastened to assure me, realizing

with dismay he may have crushed the old woman's pride, "it's great you can run. Really it is. I mean wow—you're the fastest ole lady I know."

Thanks for clearing that up kid. I feel SO MUCH better.

In any case, it was a good day. The cattle were brought home safe and sound, our family shared once more in a time of work and play, and Kayden learned something more about life on the farm.

More than that, of course, he learned what shouldn't be said to not-quite-over-the-hill-yet grandmothers.

Now, if I could only remember what the heck I came in here for …

Talkin' Trash

A few weeks ago, our kindergarten and Grade One classes worked together to complete an important task before winter snows covered the ground.

We picked up trash and tidied the schoolyard.

Before heading out, the kids milled restlessly around the foyer as small shoes were tied, coats were zipped, and everyone was issued protective, blue rubber gloves. They then received carefully enunciated instructions (that 85 percent of them missed since they were too absorbed in applying the gloves).

Once that was all taken care of, we moved in a boisterous, energetic crowd to the door, with only one minor casualty. (You can't get 20 kids out one exit without some sort of disaster). Amid wild cries of glee, they spread out across the playground, their teacher and I in hot pursuit.

Us grownups carried garbage bags, and opened them often; each time with quiet ceremony and thanks.

We covered every inch of their playground that day and I can cheerfully say that even the most minuscule scraps of paper were leapt upon with squeals of triumph and lifted on high to be proudly dropped in the bag.

However, after a time, with so much enthusiastic searching, pickings slimmed and the troops commenced to bickering amongst themselves over who had found the biggest or best piece of garbage.

A point system was instituted by one intrepid young fellow and, in a moment's time, he became judge and jury for the masses.

Fragments of crumbling chocolate wrappers were eagerly held next to shredded chip bag remains, and measurements were taken. Defeat was felt keenly, as the losers turned away to search vainly for something better with which to win the judge's approval. Suddenly I was inundated with the bark off a fir tree, handfuls of dry leaves, armloads of sticks and assorted stones.

"Hold it!" I hollered as an enterprising young girl puffed to my side with a 10-pound rock and struggled to heft it into the sack.

"Stop!" I cried again as a little fellow labored toward me under the weight of a five-foot sapling. "Trees and boulders aren't garbage."

The disappointed crowd turned sorrowfully away, and casting dark looks back over their shoulders scuffled dispiritedly at the earth.

How could they win now? SHE had ruined everything.

Suddenly a small herd of boys rushed toward me from the sidelines. "Teacher!" they cried in full voice, "we got some GOOD garbage."

"Holy smoke, what is it," I muttered anxiously. They arrived, panting breathlessly and Johnny, with great pomp and circumstance, opened his cupped hands. There, its claws curled in death, beak open in a final, unuttered chirp, a small, gray sparrow lay cold and stiff upon the little blue gloves.

"Can I hold him?" the others began to clamor excitedly.

"In a word—no," I said tonelessly.

Opening the bag, I motioned, and the small bird suffered his last indignity on this good earth as he was dropped sadly within.

Nonetheless, (although I'm sure the bird would not agree) this day was not a total loss. Johnny won.

A True Cowboy

Last Saturday morning, as my brother and I met at Dad's for our weekly family visit, I couldn't help but notice a long tear down one side of Bill's jacket.

His eyes followed mine, and he acknowledged ruefully, "Yeah, it was a fence. I'll have to ask dad to stitch it up."

This may sound like an unusual statement to make when referencing your father, but it's true—our Dad's a closet seamstress.

Well, that's a bit of an exaggeration. He sews for three reasons: he dislikes anyone buying new clothes if old ones can be repaired, his son and daughter are inept, and he alone can run the machine.

I'm not implying he could whip up a floor-length evening gown from a bolt of pink chiffon or anything, I'm just saying if you need something sewn up so solidly it won't rip again until the end of time, he's your man.

I learned that the hard way. Once I took him an expensive beige skirt that had torn up the back after I took a nasty tumble on some ice.

"Sure, I can fix it!" Dad declared, with a gleam in his eye. He returned it with a hunk of blue denim, he'd cut from an old pant leg, stitched on the inside as "reinforcement".

Then, he'd gone over and over the entire area, zigzagging with a coarse black thread, until it looked as though moles had invaded the formerly classy garment.

My eyes grew large as he demonstrated its durability now.

"See that?" he questioned proudly, yanking at the material beyond reasonable endurance. "It'll never tear again."

However, before you wrongly picture my father in a housewifely capacity: darning socks by the fire, or preparing mince tarts in a frilly apron, allow me to tell you of a time two winters ago.

It was a bitterly cold night as Dad dumped a bale of hay into a feeder, and backed out of the bull pen. He climbed from his tractor to cut strings on the bale as the young animals leapt, kicking and bunting one another. Suddenly, one jostled him; he lost his footing, and pitched forward just as a bull lashed out.

Dad was struck on the side of his head, sending him whirling back and crashing to the ground! He lay a few moments, dazed, but clambering to his feet, doggedly continued his work. The animals needed to be fed and the tractor put away.

He readied the bale, scaled a six-foot fence, shut the gate and drove the tractor back to the shed. Only then did he notice blood dripping down his coat, and put a hand up to feel his ear. It was nearly torn off.

It took a lot of persuasion to get him medical attention. "It's only a flesh wound," he protested, "I'll be fine."

Later, though, the doctor who saw him marveled at dad's grit, strength and resilience. "Your father is tough," he said with a smile. "One of the true old cowboys."

How many men, of any age, could be kicked in the head by a bull and, bleeding profusely, go on to finish up their day's work? Not many I'm sure, and very few men 87 years old.

So, from bull wrangler to seamstress, I think he's one pretty amazing fellow.

That's my dad.

Sing Me Back Home

Has it been two years?

According to the little card that arrived in my mailbox, it has, so I'll make my optometrist appointment and squint obligingly at the big letter E.

I haven't had new glasses for a while so it's probably due, but at least the choosing of new frames won't be fraught with the blushing embarrassment that accompanied a previous visit.

Poor eyesight runs in our family. We all wear glasses, even my Uncle Don, who visited one summer with his wife Esther and his ever-present guitar.

He's had a band and played old-time country music for as long as I can remember. The talent and personality he brings to his performance endears him to people, and with his longish dark hair, beard, and black Stetson, he's often told how much he resembles country music legend, Waylon Jennings.

If my son Justin or I are with him, Don always has us sing with him, which is great for Justin, a musician himself, but I'm a little reclusive and usually drag my feet. In any case, my Uncle was staying with me when, unexpectedly, he found himself in dire need of glasses.

We glided to a smooth stop outside the optician's store in my Uncle's long, black 1989 Lincoln and stepped onto the sidewalk. Esther, with her swaying, waist-length blonde hair and fringe leather jacket, Don in a long black duster, tipping a Stetson low over his eyes against the noonday sun, and I, nondescript niece, paced majestically into the shop.

The owner looked a little taken aback as we loomed in the doorway, but recovered quickly to inquire how he might be of service.

Don got straight to the point, and moved to try on the first pair of glasses he saw.

"Has anyone told you how much you look like Waylon Jennings?" the man interjected, after eyeing Don in the mirror for several long moments. "He's one of my favorite singers."

A thoughtful furrow deepened on my Uncle's brow as he paused and slowly turned from his perusal of wire frames.

"As a matter of fact they have," he said. "Say, here's a thought. I do a few of his songs. What about I sing you a couple right now for a percentage off the price of some new specs?"

If the man was taken aback before, he was flabbergasted now. "Well—I guess so," he stammered. Then suddenly he grinned, "Why not."

"Fine, fine," Don beamed, rubbing his hands together with invisible soap. "And hey! We have Jessi Colter to sing too!" (Jessi sang duets with Waylon). He rounded on me gleefully as I shrank behind a rack of sunglasses.

"Run get my guitar, Helen."

I trudged to the vehicle. "What the heck just happened in there?" I moaned. One minute we were regular Joes—normal, run-of-the-mill people out to purchase a simple pair of spectacles on a warm autumn day, and the next moment we're Country/Western singers performing an impromptu variety show in the middle of the optician's office! How do weird things like this always happen to me?

Resignedly, I reappeared with the trusty guitar, Don deftly tuned it and we were off.

Glowing red with mortification, I watched as passersby on the street stopped abruptly to press their faces against the windows for a better view of this odd exhibition, and unsuspecting patrons of the establishment trod through the door on a humble quest for eye-wear, only to halt in astonishment as we belted out a rendition of Storms Never Last. Sigh.

"That's what happens when you're related to a big star," Don chuckled, as we motored home later, once commemorative pictures were taken and hearty handshakes exchanged. Yup, it'll probably be a big let-down when I pop in for glasses alone now. "Where's Waylon?" they'll say, looking hopefully behind me.

There'll be no guitar and no singing—but great memories—you bet.

Ignorance is Bliss

There's something scary lurking in my kitchen.

It wasn't frightening in the beginning, when the world was young and it stood proud and erect on the grocery shelf, but over the passage of time it changed, warping beyond recognition.

I'm speaking, of course, of the food items we all have skulking in the darkness behind the eggs on the bottom shelf of the refrigerator, or squatting in darkened cupboards back of the cornflakes.

Maybe it's that steak sauce no one liked, but was too expensive to throw out. Perhaps it's those two wizened pickles, swaying drunkenly in their aged brine every time the fridge door is opened. Or possibly it's an ancient box of yucky banana flavored pudding mix, crouching in your pantry as it did in mine, until one gray evening when it was brought forth from the shadows by an innocent man, and consumed with great enjoyment. This despite an animated lecture from his teenage daughter on the perils of eating foods past their prime.

At least, I hope I'm not alone in occasionally keeping items a mite longer than they should be kept?

This whole unpleasant issue was bandied about our kitchen again last night by our daughter, who periodically checks the expiry dates on the food we eat, mainly because she doesn't trust us not to poison her.

It all started when she needed three tablespoons of rice wine vinegar for some exotic recipe she was making.

I felt quite pleased to inform her I had such a bottle, and directed her where to find it. Pulling it from the storeroom, she looked at me skeptically and turned it slowly in the light, searching for the best-before date.

"I'm not using this! It expired in 2007. That's 12 years ago!" she cried in shock and alarm, thrusting the offending vessel toward me.

Granted, the liquid did seem a little murky, but I protested as she moved toward the fridge like a girl possessed, and began a systematic examination of every item within. Grimly she thrust some HP sauce under my nose, bottled in 2013, vigorously shook a carton of mustard that rattled ominously, and tossed a blackened container of horseradish into the trash.

"Have we been eating this crap?" she snarled. "It's a wonder we're not all dead."

Her father and I tried reasoning with her. We explained ours was a different era. It's hard for us to throw things out. Besides, we said with conviction, those expiry dates are more like suggestions than decrees. She shook her head sorrowfully and turned away. We were hopeless.

Thankfully, things calmed down after her first rampage.

Until last night.

Passing through the kitchen, she caught sight of her father stirring his steaming banana pudding at the stove. He hummed a little tune; happily anticipating the treat he'd found lying forlornly on a shelf. She snatched up the box and scanned it.

"MOM!" she hollered. "Do you realize Dad is about to ingest a pudding that's older than me? A dessert that, should it wish, is old enough to go into a bar and order a drink," she spluttered in outrage. "In fact, this stupid dessert could have legally driven a car for the past three years! But, it's your funeral," she cried, stomping to her bedroom in disgust.

Tom looked up from his bowl with mild surprise, before bending to his spoon once more, and I shuffled back to my computer.

She should leave well enough alone.

Sometimes ignorance is bliss.

Is There a Problem?

When you think of problems common to all who dwell in the country, what two words spring to mind? That's right! Water and sewer it is. Everyone has a horror story to share; especially ones that occur in winter.

Here's mine.

For the last two months we've only had a trickle of water issuing from our taps. We have an artesian well, which flows year round and can be challenging to deal with. This year, ice built up over the lid until it became a veritable glacier; several feet deep and extending downhill toward the creek.

Children would come to visit and spend the entire day frolicking upon its banks. A more enterprising family might have charged admission, but that would have required the installation of a lift so forget it. This thing was BIG alright—trust me.

However, it was at the end of November things really took a turn for the worse. The pump, bringing cold, delicious water into our home, died. Naturally, it was down the well under four feet of solid ice.

Thankfully the flow of water didn't quit entirely, but it became necessary to plan well in advance if you wanted any.

Statements often ran like this, "I'm thirsty. Let's see—

if I turn the tap on now, I could probably have a drink tomorrow morning," or "OK, I'll be there in an hour. Just gotta rinse my hands." Heaven forbid you should want to use the toilet! It took days to recover from such an event.

Enter, a mouse. An insignificant, unrelated issue you may think, but no. This particular varmint wormed his way into the furnace ducts (wishing to take funeral arrangements into his own paws) and kicked the bloody bucket. Suddenly, with every sickening breath, we began to physically absorb the remains of a rotting rodent. Peachy.

If you can forgive the expression, this is where the waters really got muddied.

At the height of our suffering, family from Manitoba called to say they were coming for a visit. Foolishly, they showed up at our door with big smiles and the expectation of country hospitality. Hmm—how to break the news?

"Welcome to the farm," we trilled, enveloping them in a warm embrace. Then, stepping back, I assumed the stance of a drill sergeant and barked, "OK PEOPLE, PIPE DOWN AND LISTEN UP. You can't have a drink, wash your face, or flush the toilet. Here's a roll of toilet paper and a pail, use it wisely. You're welcome to brush your teeth with orange juice like we do, but there's absolutely no bathing unless you want to trudge outside and roll about on that heap of ice in the backyard."

Rigidly, they filed past, faces registering shock and alarm as I continued. "Oh, and by the way—that cloying stench of death lingering in the air is a decomposing rat lying somewhere in the ventilation system—try not to breathe any more than you have to."

Sometimes gracious country living isn't all it's cracked up to be I guess, but we love it despite the problems involved.

As our company disappeared around the corner I lovingly uttered one last, loud word of caution gained from unhappy personal experience, "And whatever you do, DON'T KNOCK OVER THE PEE POT!"

Those Who Live in Glass Houses

While in Edmonton having dinner with good friends, Cyndi and Darrell, recently, I recounted several humorous tales from a long-ago visit made to mutual friends living on Vancouver Island.

They were a lovely couple whose parents, like so many others, had come to Canada for the promise of land and the opportunity to forge a new way of life. Our friends had inherited that land, working hard on it their whole lives through, and retired finally to a well-earned rest in a milder climate.

The lady in question was a thrifty soul who, during the '30s, had learned to waste NOTHING—sometimes to the point of ridiculousness.

I recall visiting them once while suffering with a sore throat. From somewhere at the back of a kitchen cupboard she produced an old rumpled package of Fisherman's Friend lozenges—the extra strong variety—and insisted I take one.

Bleh. I accepted warily, not wishing to offend, but as wave after wave of the powerful mentholated fumes hit my brain, causing the hair on my head to stand up and salute, I discreetly spat the whole nasty business into the trash.

It was reminiscent of a scene from a late night horror flick when, returning later for a glass of water, I spied the very same lozenge on a plate by the sink.

"How did this get here?" I asked her in amazement, as she bustled about the kitchen. For an answer she popped it into her mouth and crunched it down. She couldn't bear to see anything wasted, and rescuing the sticky brown lump from atop a few coffee grounds, she rinsed it off and ate it herself.

"But you don't even have a cold," I protested, as she peered at me through watering eyes.

Another time I noticed her soak the porridge pot after breakfast and then carefully scrape any traces of oatmeal residue and flakes of hardened glip that clung to the rim of the pan, into a bowl. These congealed, gray, lumps of sludge were then covered and placed into the refrigerator.

What the heck?

I asked her to clarify this strange practice and she explained happily that at the close of each week there would be enough of the remains to prepare a lovely dessert.

A little sugar, some vanilla, a few eggs, a dash of milk and *voila*! Porridge pudding. YIKES!

Later that day, during my visit with Cyndi, we stopped for lunch. While delicious, my meal didn't have enough salt (it's my vice, don't judge). I asked for some. They didn't have packets available, so a woman in the back poured a small measure into a disposable plastic container.

As we prepared to leave, I stared at the small dish beside me. There was still plenty of salt left and I'd enjoyed it. Who knew when I might need some again? Besides, it was wasteful to throw it away. Snapping on the lid, I bundled it into my purse.

"Interesting," Cyndi said quietly, once outside the door, "Interesting that you should be snickering at the frugality of others."

"What are you saying?" I retorted defensively, clutching my handbag close, and the dash of salt that lurked within.

But of course, I knew exactly what she meant. I hate when she's right.

A Series of Unpleasant Events

Ever had one of those days—a day that's trouble from beginning to end?

I experienced one early this winter, and have decided to take you along for the whole miserable re-enactment. Lucky you.

It all began with a few harmless goodies I'd prepared the night before. They were chocolate and needed to chill, so I popped them outside, high on a shelf by the door. Next morning I slipped out to start my school bus and saw the container broken and empty, cookies strewn about hither and yon, while Chili, our dog, gnawed on one at the foot of the stairs.

Sheesh, how fast can a dog work? She'd only been let out five minutes ago. I bent to wrench it from her slavering jaws. Knowing chocolate isn't good for dogs, I felt relieved it was frozen solid and she hadn't gotten much. Quickly I found the others and carried them all back inside.

On my second attempt to leave, I could see the annoying hound lying on the driveway in the darkness; head bent, paws holding the morsel tightly as her teeth ground into yet another one.

Blast that dog! This time she was a little savvier. Reluctant to hand over her spoils, she capered off across the lawn.

Yay, a game!

At length, I wrestled it from her mouth with my bare hands and irritably carried the dripping mass back to the house.

Carelessly, I glanced at it in the porch lights glow.

ACK!" I screeched, dropping the slimy, brown, hunk of CAT CRAP in revulsion.

Horror number one.

Later that afternoon I pulled the bus back into my yard and sat for a moment, glad to be home. I reached into my pocket for the house key. Not there. Tried my other pocket, tried my bag, and then tried each door. Nothing.

Being the impatient person I am, I slumped onto the steps thinking of ways to break in.

A sudden grin lit my face as I marched to the shed and lugged back a 20-foot ladder. It slammed against the eves with a crunch, but all appeared well. I envisioned myself easily reaching out to slide open the window and nimbly clambering inside.

It was not to be. Unless I was prepared to launch myself into mid-air and bridge a gap of about five feet from ladder to window, it wasn't going to happen. Plus, it would be a cute trick to hover there, defying the laws of gravity, whilst working the window open prior to entry.

Next plan was to hike over to Dad's place and find a shorter ladder in the tractor shed. The door was unlocked, which was odd, but handy. I pushed it open a crack.

"Hellooo," I called, not wishing to startle the men as they labored over machinery repairs. No answer. I pushed the door open a little further, stepped in and fumbled for the switch. Flipping it on I looked up to seek my prize and met the wide, accusing glare of a dead deer suspended by its heels from the tines of a bale handler.

"AAAH!" I screamed, lunging back in alarm and tumbling into a pile of used tractor rags. In a stiff breeze from the open door, the carcass began sadly to sway to and fro, its bulbous eyes following my every move. With a tortured moan I rushed from the building, slammed the door, and leaned on the wall outside to calm my racing heart. Drat son Chris and his evil, hunting ways.

Horror number two.

"Hey," I thought, brightening a bit as I trudged back to Dads. (I'd given up on the break and enter thing once the horned specter of death stared me down.) "I'll find the Christmas decorations while I wait."

Each year I store several large boxes of them up in dad's attic since I don't have space. Mounting the steep staircase, I began dragging the cumbersome tubs to the door, checking each one. It was as I tore a lid off the second box that a putrid odor began to penetrate the room.

"What the heck?" I exclaimed, unwisely rummaging

through it. Each item was pulled forth and immediately set aside in a choking cloud of rot. Finally, I dragged up a handily tied grocery bag and lifted it for inspection.

"Oh no," I said grimly, casting my thoughts backward in time to a cold winter's day last January. Back to a day when the tree had been dismantled, decorations packed and I'd uttered several key words, "Tom, have you seen that tub of ice cream and pound of bacon I just bought? How could they vanish into thin air?" Now, I knew how.

Horror number three.

So there you have it. Pretty nasty, right?

However, apart from my decorations, there really wasn't any harm done. Unless, of course, you count the irreparable damage done to my delicate psyche over this series of unpleasant events.

Tell Me a Story

Learning to write an interesting story isn't always easy for young children.

Oh, they know one when they read one of course, but it's a complicated matter to put it together for themselves.

There are the bothersome mechanics of: punctuation, grammar and capitalization, developing the plot and then bringing it to some sort of logical conclusion. But that doesn't stop kids from doing it however they please, usually with a blatant disregard for such irritants.

Often, I have the privilege of assisting in this process, and while I'm hardly an expert, I do love helping them develop some skill at it, and feel good about their accomplishments.

Recently, the children in our Grade 2 class learned how to write a legend. They told fascinating tales of how: the *Porcupine Got His Quills, The Horse Found His Neigh,* and *Rabbits Learned to Hop.*

These were, indeed, riveting accounts, but the one I'm best acquainted with is: *How the Snake Lost His Legs.* It contained a short, grisly summary of this timeless event; its simple message holding the reader spellbound as we read how the snake lost his many appendages during a vicious attack perpetrated by a wandering iguana.

Allow me to offer up a brief synopsis of the whole sordid story, and it's rather abrupt/cliff-hanger ending.

There was this snake, see, and one day he decided to go for a stroll along a sunny dirt road. (Sometimes the worst possible crimes take place along sunny dirt roads, particularly if you're a snake). Anyway, this nameless serpent was out rambling hither and yon, minding his own business and exercising his freedom to stride freely upon the path of life. Suddenly, out from bloody nowhere, leapt a maniacal iguana wielding a long, gleaming knife!

"Ha-ha!" the iguana screamed crazily, before lunging at the unsuspecting snake and slashing feverishly at his vulnerable legs. (I told you this was grisly didn't I?)

Then, concluding his fearsome raid upon the innocent snake, the iguana mysteriously disappeared, never to be seen again.

Naturally, this leaves us questioning the motive for such a violent strike. What inexplicable forces were at work in the pea-sized brain of the lizard? What dastardly scheme was at the heart of such rage? Alas, we shall never know, for now enters a rat. The End.

"OK, wait a moment," I exclaimed in surprise, flipping the page to check if more was scribbled on the back. Nope. I turned to question the tiny author beside me. "That's it? But you can't just have some random rat scamper in and call it a day. What happened to the snake?"

She shrugged her shoulders and stared listlessly across

the room, "I dunno," she said dismissively. "That's the end. I don't know what happened next."

I shook my head in bewilderment. How to help her understand? "But if you don't know—who does? You're the only one who can know. It's your story. You have to finish it."

Narrowing her eyes with irritation, she turned away and pretended to examine a crumb left over from snack time.

The creative juices had dried. I, and my foolish babblings, had become merely a nuisance to the child.

Clearly there was nothing further to be done with the dismembered reptile, and he must cut his losses and move on as best he could—evidently without the benefit of limbs. The End.

Keeping it Real

My daughter and I have been drinking a lot of cocoa lately. In fact, I was buying a small container of the chocolaty mix every week.

I say "was" because this Saturday I read the label on our usual brand and came away feeling shocked and appalled. It's really best to avoid items that are packaged or processed to the nth degree. Yes, they might be quicker, and make life easier sometimes, but there are no substitutes for real foods.

My attention had been caught as I stood in the grocery aisle and read a proud statement on the hot chocolate tin boasting, "Made with real cocoa". Well what the heck else would it be made of? Sawdust? Cat litter? Perhaps a measure of cow dung? Good grief.

Much to Aliyah's irritation, I paused to peruse the list of ingredients and found, to my dismay, that cocoa came fourth, only slightly more important than modified cellulose and silicon dioxide. YUM.

"That's it!" I announced dramatically, placing the container back on the shelf. "We have actual cocoa at home to make our drinks. No more shortcuts."

Whenever possible I believe in making recipes from scratch. Take bread for example. Almost every weekend I bake a large batch of hearty, brown bread. I add whatever takes my fancy at the moment: rye and whole wheat flour for sure, oatmeal, Red River cereal, ground flax, all mixed up in a vat with some honey for sweetening, a little salt, oil and plenty of water.

Kayden, my grandson, was out last weekend and helped me. We made a batch of white bread, which became cinnamon buns, and another of brown. I always take some over to share with dad and often give a loaf to other family members too. A gift of fresh baked bread is never turned away.

Unless you're like my husband, of course. He doesn't care for the taste of yeast and won't eat anything made with whole wheat. Tom prefers foods that are white and innocuous, preferably ones that have a shelf life upwards of 75 years and contain a nutrient level of approximately zero.

If you can deep-fry it, flip it out of a box, or add water and serve, so much the better.

Not that he isn't a good cook. Among other things, he makes a dandy beef soup with fresh vegetables and pearl barley, and from time to time turns out some mean chili. Also, he can sort through his selection of mixes and whip up Creamy Garlic Fettuccine in ten minutes flat.

In fact, he absolutely insists on making this dish himself because he believes it to be superior to my recipe, which foolishly requires the use of real garlic, onions, cream and grated Parmesan cheese.

What a nut I was to think I could compete with such appealing ingredients as sodium phosphate, glucose solids and that delectable old favorite, xanthan gum. Helen you complete blockhead.

In any case, this concludes my tirade for today. I've worked myself up into a bit of a lather over it all.

Guess I'd better sit down, take a few deep breaths, and drink a nice hot coffee laced with…wait, what's this? No cream? All that's left to use is Tom's fake, edible oil product?

I feel another rant coming on.

Lost and Found

We haven't had water to wash clothes at our house lately, which has forced me to bundle everything up in baskets and trundle it off to a Laundromat. I like Laundromats.

There's something relaxing about slouching in a warm room with a good book and the continual hum of dryers. It's quite a rewarding experience, although I have to say I take a certain amount of undeserved flack over how I handle the machines. My husband doesn't trust me with his socks.

Yes, you heard me—socks.

Personally I think he has a bit of a hang-up with the unassuming garment, but you can't argue with City Hall. He says I lose them, and I figure his whole gripe is ridiculous. If they go missing it's nothing to do with me, but my protestations fall on deaf ears. I tell him: clearly the appliance consumed them for reasons of its own or perhaps the malodorous footwear got up and left of its own accord. Either way—not my problem, but he doesn't buy it.

Sometimes, weeks later, they turn up for no apparent reason at the bottom of his designated drawer, or under the bed which, in some bizarre turn of events, is also my fault. I can't win. I bet the man owns over 40 sets of them anyway! What's one pair, more or less?

In any case, each friendless sock ends up in my lost and

found hamper, waiting indefinitely for its mate.

We have a lost and found bin at school too.

Recently I saw our vice-principal sorting through the abandoned articles flung within. Carefully she folded each item neatly and laid it on a table so parents or children could easily retrieve their missing apparel. A few mismatched mittens, several shapeless toques, endless numbers of hoodies and even an assortment of shoes were drawn forth and set aside to be showcased in the foyer.

However, it was as Tina held aloft a pair of small trousers that she paused and turned to me with a confused shake of her head and a bemused look in her eyes.

"I can understand losing a hat, some mitts, or a hoodie," Tina said, almost to herself as she grappled with this mystifying dilemma. "What I don't understand is how you can leave without your pants?"

She next held up some jeans, and brushed an imaginary speck of lint from one knee. "I mean, these were left during the winter. It was cold outside, right? Who walks out into the snow without their pants on?" She turned back to the tub and uncovered a third pair. "Does this make any sense to you Helen? Seriously—does it?"

Not really expecting a reply for a riddle to which there was no solution, she continued in her self-appointed task, still muttering. "Pants? I just don't get it…"

Some questions in life simply have no good answer. We

can't know or comprehend why things are the way they are; our lot in life is to accept what we cannot change without endless, grudging complaint.

And so, with that in mind I say, "Get over it Tom."

Filling the Cookie Jar

Cookies have been a welcome addition at festivals and holiday rituals for as long as baking has been recorded, and it's a custom continued to this day. Everyone has his or her favorites.

For some a buttery shortbread is the answer while others enjoy spicing things up with some gingerbread. If you're like me, you might prefer something laced with chocolate and nuts.

During this festive season, every gathering seems to harbor a plate or two of the delicious morsels. Any way you slice it, cookies are a tasty and traditional part of Christmas.

One December, my dear friend Cyndi and I decided to combine efforts and spend a fun-filled day together baking holiday treats. We drew up an extensive list with foolish confidence in our ability to accomplish everything in an afternoon. Prior to this event, however, Cyndi fell prey to some slick advertising on the cover of a glossy magazine featuring directions on how to construct an "Old English" gingerbread cottage with thatched roof in "five simple steps."

"It looks easy Helen!" she enthused, brimming with the cool self-assurance of a rank amateur.

I arrived at her door that morning, my arms laden

with the usual baking ingredients: chocolate, flour, butter, sugar—did I mention chocolate?

Lightheartedly laughing in anticipation of the fruitful day ahead, we fell to work amid the happy clatter of pans. Her large, pristine kitchen gleamed in the morning sun as we briskly bustled about our many, many tasks. Fools!

After a laborious day of loaves, fudge, tarts, cookies and squares Cyndi had only started rolling the gingerbread by 5 o'clock; a dark, evil looking concoction cracking repeatedly under the strain of preparation. I poked fitfully at an unpleasant mass in the bottom of a saucepan, which bubbled angrily; not unlike some Shakespearean cauldron brewing a foul potion.

Clouds of flour had settled in our hair, aging us before our time. Streaks of some ungodly, unknown mixture decorated our faces and we stumbled occasionally on weakened limbs as we trod to and fro on nasty, sticky clumps of glip that littered the floor of her filthy premises.

Leaning heavily on the sink, I gazed at my friend through the acrid haze of burned tarts and said, "There's a lesson to be learned here."

Further to this fiasco—the crowning achievement of the day—was the English country cottage in five easy steps. It had, in fact, become a terrifying apparition in 67. The hateful magazine had included photos of a glistening kitchen and beaming first prize winner standing proudly beside her beautifully appointed structure.

Cyndi stood amongst the rubble of her pantry, grim determination etched on her face as, in a final gesture of defeat, she plugged in her hot glue gun and resolutely welded it together.

Muttering darkly to herself concerning idiot prize winners, she lavishly plastered shredded wheat to the roof with a second round of mucilage, pushed hopefully at a wall drooping almost perpendicular to the table, and stood back to squint at it with listless eyes.

Turning towards me she spread her hands in resignation, "It doesn't look anything like an English cottage—it looks like a deserted African hut from the pages of an old National Geographic magazine."

Yes, our favorite holiday treats may take on many forms, but as long as memories are made and good times are shared, you can overlook a little glue here and there.

Christmas cookies are an enduring tradition to be enjoyed by one and all. Get baking!

Trouble for Santa

Twas Christmas Eve as Santa,
Lumbered gladly from his bed.
Kissed the little woman,
And made sure the cat was fed.

Then sliding on his slippers,
Hurried off with measured stride.
Across to yonder window,
Where he took a look outside.

The elves were busy working,
As they fed and hitched the team.
So Santa ate his porridge,
Thickly laced with sugared cream.

He washed it down with coffee,
Twenty biscuits and some cake.
Oatmeal cookies, crispy waffles,
Pumpkin pie and chocolate shake.

Then, sighing rather loudly,
Santa loosened off his belt.
Being chubby was his trademark!
There were others to look svelte.

"It's ready," Sparky bellowed,
Leaning in through Santa's door.
But Santa only nodded,
As he toyed with eating more.

Reluctantly he gathered,
Up his coat, his mitts, his hat,
And waddled to the kitchen,
Where his lovely wife was sat.

Concerned he might feel peckish,
Mrs. Claus had made a lunch,
And reaching down to grab it,
Santa whispered, "Thanks a bunch."

He threw it to his shoulder,
As he hastened to the sleigh,
But, as he hopped aboard it,
Santa's crimson pants gave way!

They made a fearful rending,
As they tore from stem to stern.
And dropped around his ankles,
(Causing Santa's face to burn).

A gasp went up about him.
Elvish faces turned away.
They couldn't bear to see him,
With his pants in disarray.

Till Sparky, ever helpful,
Bounded in to Santa's aid.
He'd always worked for Santa,
(Though the elf had ne're been paid).

"I'll save you," Sparky hollered,
And he tore his small coat off,
Ran up to cover Santa,
But then, with an awkward cough…

He noticed that his jacket,
Was for sure too small to work,
And several of the reindeer,
Bent their heads to hide a smirk.

Soon, every elf came dashing,
Just to see what they could do.
The pants were pinned and stapled. Yikes!
(They even tried some glue).

But no one could repair them.
There was nothing could be done.
So Santa, in his boxers,
Sadly said, "Well, it's been fun."

"But I can't fly the midnight sky,
Or leap down chimney's hot,
In nothing more than cotton briefs!
Nope — Christmas Eve is shot."

Then Sparky led the others,
In a call for Mrs. Claus.
Where, rushing to the rescue,
She was met with wild applause.

The elves stood back in wonder,
As she peered at Ole St. Nick,
And making a decision cried,
"Go get my ball gown. QUICK!"

She snipped, and fussed and stitched it,
Wrapping fabric round his girth.
Till Santa stood resplendent
And the elves collapsed in mirth.

They toppled into snow banks,
Rolling round and round the square.
They giggled and they chortled
Till he fixed them with a glare.

For Santa, in this getup,
Had now lost his manly pride,
"Looks great!" insisted Sparky,
But of course the elf had lied.

So Santa, thus attired,
Thanked his wife and turned to walk.
(Although it wasn't easy,
To maneuver in a frock).

He whistled to his reindeer,
Jumped headlong into the sleigh,
And with the presents loaded,
They rose up and flew away.

Yet, before he made his exit,
I could clearly hear him yell,
"The velvet dress is one thing,

But… THESE PANTYHOSE ARE HELL!"

Helen Row Toews is a writer, works in education, and carries a license to drive anything on wheels (stilettos and lipstick optional).

Living on the family farm near Marshall, Saskatchewan, Helen shares her love of the Canadian Prairies, family, travel and country living—all humorously woven into the fabric of these memorable tales. Her fondest wish is to bring a smile to your face.

Other Prairie Wool Books by Helen Row Toews include *Great, Just Great?*

If you long to travel the world, dream of life in the country, or waste nights wondering what fulfillment could be found as the proud driver of a manure truck, fantasize no longer: Helen's got you covered as she takes you from the streets of Paris to the cowsheds of Saskatchewan, all without changing her shoes.

Manufactured by Amazon.ca
Acheson, AB